Elsa

A historical novel about love, survival,
and making choices in a Canadian mining town

Nettie Leeflang

www.nettieleeflang.com

Proverbs 16:9

A man's heart plans his way,

but the Lord directs his steps.

Elsa

Other books by Nettie Leeflang
Hitchhiker, Dutch version, 2019
Hitchhiker, English version, 2024

Elsa
Copyright 2025 © Nettie G. Leeflang
Cover photo credit: Cottonbro Studio on Pexels.com
www.nettieleeflang.com
All rights reserved.
ISBN 978-1-0689861-4-7

First printed in Dutch by:
© Uitgeverij De Banier, Apeldoorn 2024
Omslagontwerp en vormgeving: Albert Bloemert
ISBN 978 94 0291 1268
C-NUR 342
www.debanier.nl

Foreword

Have you heard? Mount Sicker is on fire."
I look at Patricia, in shock.
The summer of 2021 is sweltering hot. The thermometer reaches 40 degrees at the peak of the day, and I've never experienced temperatures like this before. Moreover, it hasn't rained in seven weeks, creating a perfect recipe for a forest fire.
"You didn't know?" Patricia asks, surprised.
I shake my head and wipe the sweat from my face.
"Why didn't I see any smoke coming from Mount Prevost?" I wonder aloud. I'm at a survival group meeting that I attend every two weeks. On the way here, I had a view of Mount Prevost, the mountain in front of Mount Sicker. Apparently, I was so lost in thought that I didn't notice the smoke.
"A large number of firefighters have been deployed. Two firefighting planes are working alongside the fire trucks to get the blaze under control," Patricia says.
I think of my friends who live on Mount Sicker Road and Small Mount Sicker. How are they? Have they had to evacuate? Are they safe? I search my bag for my phone, only to realize I had left it at home.
Suddenly, my curiosity overtakes my concern. Could the fire reveal treasures once again, just as it did 120 years back? Let me tell you what happened here more than a century ago.

Vancouver, 1881

There's a letter from Paul," I call out, waving the envelope in my hand as I step through the front door. Wonderful aromas greet me from the kitchen, where Sarah, our maid, is cooking. My two little sisters, Rose and Jasmin, both six years old, come running down the hall to greet me. I hug them and head into the living room. Dad is already home for dinner, sitting in his armchair by the fireplace, while Kate, my adopted sister who is older than me by one year, is on the couch, embroidering. Mom is placing the cutlery next to the plates. They all look up in surprise.

"I stopped by the post office on my way home from school to check for any letters or packages," I explain.

"Hurry," Mom says nervously, "sit down." She pulls up a chair for me by the fireplace. "Read the letter out loud."

I sit down, and the twins climb onto my lap. I tear a strip from the short side of the envelope and pull out a thick stack of densely written pages. Laughing, I say, "This looks like something a journalist would do—so many pages!"

"You mean it's just like your boyfriend would do," Rose says with her spontaneous childlike wisdom.

I blush. "Shh," I say, pretending to be annoyed.

Rose and Jasmin giggle behind their little hands, which they hold up to their faces.

Paul's even handwriting is easy to read. I examine the pages from all sides and then start reading from the first sheet.

Dear Hawthorn Family,

As I write this letter, it's April 1881. This morning, as usual, I took a walk along the beach at Port Saint John, notebook and pen in hand. The South African sun had just risen, casting its light over the ocean. Behind me, the low buildings of the village stood nestled between the trees. Everything was still quiet, save for the gentle crash of waves on the shore. I selected a spot with a good view of the passage between the mountains toward the ocean, waiting, like everyone else, for the arrival of the ship that would take us to the Cape of Good Hope. My pen swirled over the blank page, but no words came. I had already written about everything that had happened recently.

I dozed off and was later roused by the sounds of the village awakening. The sun had climbed high in the sky. I stood up and stretched in its warm rays, noticing that the first noisy customers had arrived at the tavern. My attention was drawn to a movement at the edge of the forest. Someone was emerging from the undergrowth. I didn't recognize the man who, leaning on a crooked stick, stumbled out of the woods. I hurried over to him. His clothes were dirty and torn, and he wore what remained of a British army uniform. His beard was matted and grimy, and from his eyes, I could tell he was no older than twenty.

"Can I help you, sir?" I asked, my concern evident.

"Sir?" the man growled from beneath his mud-caked helmet, which must have once been white. "Since when are you calling me 'sir'?"

The voice sounded familiar, and with a shock, I realized who I was looking at.

"Come with me," I said, grabbing the sleeve of his tattered jacket.

He pulled his arm away. "I can walk just fine by myself. You don't need to drag me," he grumbled.

He hasn't changed a bit, I thought, and together, we made our way to the tavern where I knew the other soldiers would be. I opened the door to the inn and called into the dimly lit room, "Look who we have here."

The murmur in the pub fell silent. The men who were already there turned their heads toward the door. Then came a thunderous cheer. Half-full glasses were raised in the air, and the newcomer was invited to the large table in the middle of the room. The soldiers slapped him on the shoulder, and though I saw him flinch, he made no sound. Was he in pain or just exhausted? Someone ordered beer for the young man, who drank it down in greedy gulps, prompting the landlord to refill his glass immediately.

"Tell us," the men urged.

I moved closer to the group around the table. This would make a great follow-up story for the Vancouver Weekly Herald, for which I write.

The beer on the ragged man's empty stomach had the expected effect. He began to boast, his words growing increasingly inflated. I wasn't surprised that he hadn't improved; in fact, he seemed even meaner than I remembered.

I struggled to make sense of his rambling. The men around the table listened intently, but their half-drunk minds seemed to grasp little of the story.

Yet the arrival of the lost soldier was a welcome diversion in the otherwise dull wait for a ship to take us farther. Later, I told myself, I would speak with him again when the effects of the beer had worn off and he could converse more coherently. But first, let me tell you what led up to this unexpected reunion with the soldier.

"Who is this soldier?" Mom asks anxiously.
"I don't know, Mom," I reply. "Should I keep reading? We'll probably find out soon."
"Do that, Elsa," Dad encourages.
He is perched on the edge of his armchair, his newspaper forgotten on the table beside him. Kate's face reflects the same tension we all feel. It's hard for us to accept that three of the boys we grew up with have gone off to fight with the British against the Boers in South Africa. Every Sunday at church, we see the worry etched on the faces of their families—Paul's grandmother and the parents of Dylan and Fred. We all long for an end to that dreadful war.
I pick up the next page and continue reading aloud.

Two months ago, at the end of February 1881, I silently ascended the west side of Majuba Hill alongside British soldiers. Though it was night, the moon provided enough light to see where we put our feet. Until halfway up the hill, we were shielded by trees and bushes, which offered some cover if needed. The local wildlife remained eerily silent as if waiting to see what would unfold, curious about the commotion caused by these intruding soldiers on their mountain.

As you know, the conflict between the Boers and the British government began about five months ago. In November 1880, Piet Bezuidenhout refused to pay an illegally imposed tax. In response, the government seized Piet's wagon and attempted to auction it off. However, the government underestimated the solidarity among the Boers. Approximately a hundred Boers came to Piet's aid, attacking the sheriff and reclaiming the wagon. In retaliation, British soldiers were dispatched to confront the Boers. When the British sought to annex Transvaal from the Boers in December, the war became inevitable.

We arrived in Cape Town, at the southern tip of Africa, in February after a long journey. Alongside us, 1,500 recruits from Newcastle, England, also arrived. We proceeded toward Laingsnek, where tensions between the British and the Boers were running high, with several battles already fought. I've sent reports of these confrontations to the newspaper in Vancouver, and once the mail arrives, you'll read about them in the Vancouver Weekly Herald.

Our newly arrived contingent was assigned to assist British Major General Colley in retaking the mountain pass—a crucial link between Pietermaritzburg in Natal and Pretoria in Transvaal—from the Boers. The Boers had established their camp on the far side of Majuba Hill.

"Prepare for at least three days of defending this hill," Colley had warned the British soldiers before we began our climb that night.

"This will be a piece of cake," Fred boasted to Dylan.

You know how Fred is—always loud and bragging. As usual, he thinks he knows better than the Major

General. His complaints about the food and military leadership are endless. Dylan and I usually just let him ramble.

"We're professional soldiers, and those Boers don't know anything about fighting wars. They'd be better off sticking to their cows and vegetables. The fact that they've beaten us at Bronkhorstspruit, Skuinshoogte, and last time at Laingsnek was just luck," Fred bragged.

"I'm not so sure," Dylan said cautiously. "You have to admit they're incredibly good marksmen."

"Are you saying we aren't?" Fred retorted, clearly annoyed.

"No, I'm not saying that," Dylan replied, panting as he searched for a foothold to pull himself up the hill. The climb was no picnic, and he was breathing heavily. "The Boers are always hunting wild game, like antelopes and birds. Their first shot has to hit, or their prey is gone in the dense foliage."

"We'll have the advantage of shooting down at them. You'll see, we'll mow them down," Fred insisted, trying to dismiss Dylan's concerns.

"I hope so," Dylan said breathlessly. "If we can even see them. Those blasted peasants wear clothes that blend into the landscape. Look at us with our red coats and white helmets. We're practically living targets."

"Don't let Colley hear your demotivating comments," Fred sneered.

I listened to their conversation and immediately thought of a new article idea. However, I had to be cautious with what I wrote. You never knew if Major General Colley would throw me in jail for spreading demoralizing misinformation.

I continued climbing the hill with the more than four hundred soldiers. My load was much lighter than theirs, and I carried no weapon. Halfway up, the dense vegetation gave way to bare rock, making the climb more challenging. I was concerned about how things would be when the sun was high above us—there was no cover in sight from our current position to the top of the hill.

In the distance, the sky was already turning a soft red as the sun prepared to rise above the horizon. When we reached the summit, General Colley issued his orders, and the men began to spread out across the hilltop. I selected a spot at the edge where I could overlook the valley and keep an eye on the Boer army. I was grateful not to be in the same uniform as our soldiers. My white helmet would indeed have made a perfect target for the Boer sharpshooters if I were to stick my head over the edge.

"You can rest for a while before we start the fight," Colley commanded.

After the grueling nighttime climb, the soldiers were more than willing to take a break. It was, after all, Sunday morning. Not that soldiers cared much about the Lord's Day, but everyone needed rest, whether you were a soldier or a Boer.

I sat with my back against an outcropping of rock, a little away from the soldiers. I took out my notebook from my backpack and scribbled a few notes but soon pulled my hat over my eyes and dozed off. The warmth of the rising sun was soothing, and it felt good to rest after the arduous climb before the battle began. When I opened my eyes, the sun was much higher in the sky. I sat up, pushed my hat back, and wiped the sweat from my forehead. Curiously, I looked over the edge of the hilltop into the valley. The sun shone directly into my face, and I squinted. The Boer camp appeared unusually quiet. I didn't see a single Boer moving around. It was strange; farmers typically rose with the light. In our camp too, it was quiet—most of the soldiers were sleeping in the warming sun, while a few were awake, passing the time by cleaning their rifles. I crawled back to my spot by the rock and resumed writing my article.

I had only written two sentences when I was jolted by the first nearby gunshots. The air immediately filled with shouts and cries of pain.

I ducked behind the rock and peered around the corner. The Boers were swarming into our camp over the edge of the hill. They were shooting with deadly precision at our soldiers, who fell one by one, collapsing to the ground, moaning loudly. My heart pounded like crazy, and I tried to make myself invisible behind the rock.

The Boers spread rapidly across the hill, sowing death and destruction in their wake. A few of our soldiers had the clarity of mind to return fire, but it was futile. The surprise attack of the Boers was successful. The ear-deafening gunfire and the screams and groans of the wounded seemed endless.

"Oh, God," I prayed desperately, "please let this violence stop."

Gradually, the shooting subsided. More and more groups of English soldiers, now held at gunpoint by Boers, raised their hands in surrender. The Boers herded together our soldiers who were still alive and were able to stand on their feet.

A young Boer, rifle at the ready, approached me. I raised my hands, holding my notebook and pen in a gesture of surrender.

"Don't shoot, don't shoot," I begged. "I'm a journalist." I wasn't sure if he understood me, but apparently, my attire and my "weapons" were enough to convince him I posed no threat. He gestured for me to join the group of survivors. I complied, navigating through the groaning, wounded men to join the prisoners. The group was small compared to the original number; I estimated that only a quarter of our army remained unscathed. I gazed in despair at all the bodies strewn across the hilltop.

The British weapons were gathered by a few Boers and tossed into a large pile. Our group was ordered to assist with the wounded and to gather the dead.

This was the most horrifying task I had ever faced in my life. Even the job of cleaning intestines at the butcher shop, when I worked fresh out of school, seemed trivial compared to the sight of so much pain and blood. The sun was at its highest and burned fiercely on our heads.

Behind me, I heard a lot of grumbling.

"Those filthy peasants."

It was Fred, venting his black heart to Dylan. Both were among the survivors, and their grumbling was understandable; I didn't hold it against them.

A Boer jabbed Fred with his rifle and said, "Shut up."

The scene was dreadful under the relentless sun, filled with the stench of dirt, sweat, and fear. Yet, we were still alive.

The soldiers were counted. Among the Boers, one had been killed, and seven were wounded.

The dead one was taken to a separate spot where a young Boer sat with him, his shoulders hunched and his face hidden in his hands; we were not to see his tears.

We also counted our dead and wounded: we had lost 92 soldiers, and 134 were injured. Among the dead was Major General Colley, who had been struck in the right eye by a Boer bullet, marking his end.

What would become of us now? What did these so-called barbarians do with their prisoners? Were they going to impale us on stakes, as the Zulus were known to do? The thought made me feel nauseous.

"Oh, dear," Mother laments as I pause in my reading. She wrings her hands in her lap. "Why did those boys have to go to South Africa?"

"Keep reading," Kate says impatiently. She is, of course, curious how Dylan is doing. She hasn't embroidered a stitch since I began reading the letter.

"They're probably in a prisoner-of-war camp," my father adds to the conversation. This triggers more lamenting from Mother. He tries to comfort her unsuccessfully.

"Rose," Father says, "go fetch some lavender and chamomile tea from Sarah in the kitchen."

"Why me again?" Rose grumbles with an aggrieved expression.

"I'll go," Jasmin says, standing up to head toward the kitchen.

"Jasmin," Father says firmly, "you stay here. I gave the order to Rose."

Muttering under her breath, Rose gets up.

"Wait with reading until I get back, Elsa," she says to me as she walks out of the living room.

I wait until Rose comes back and then I resume my reading.

≈

We were ordered to carry our dead and wounded to the Boer camp. Descending the hill proved just as challenging as the climb from the previous night. The dead were unwieldy, and the wounded leaned heavily on the shoulders of the healthy soldiers—of whom there were too few to assist everyone. Those who could manage somewhat on their own had to find their way down. To my surprise, the Boers assisted in carrying the wounded and the dead.

Despite our careful steps, we sometimes slid a considerable distance downhill due to the weight of our comrades. This caused a great deal of groaning and swearing from the wounded, who screamed in pain.

At the base of the mountain, the Boer camp barracks were set up made from corrugated iron, brought in with farmers' and woodcutters' wagons.

"Do we have to live in these pigsties?" Fred complained.

An older soldier decided it was time to set Fred straight. "Listen, boy," he said, "these so-called hostile Boers, as we've been told, are actually treating us well compared to what we do to them. We're the ones colonizing their land, sending their women and children into concentration camps. Even the English who try to help them are stuck in camps with no livelihood. These people are showing us more kindness than we would if the roles were reversed, understand?"

This nearly ignited a fight between Fred and the older soldier. Fortunately, a few others intervened and separated them.

We settled into the barracks as best we could, tending to the wounded and laying them on field mats. The barracks were hot and stuffy, reeking of pain, sweat, and blood. When it was quiet, and my assistance seemed no longer needed, I stepped outside for some fresh air.

I didn't want to sit idly by doing nothing, so I set out in search of new stories. On the 'street' that ran between the barracks, soldiers were lounging in the shade against the corrugated iron walls. At the end of the street stood a high chicken wire fence, with the young Boer who had spared me earlier stationed in front of it. In the distance, to his left and right, at the corners of the fence, other Boers stood guard, their eyes occasionally scanning our way to ensure I wasn't causing any trouble to their fellow soldier.

I approached the young Boer. "Thank you for not shooting me immediately when you saw me."

He grinned. "I could tell right away that you posed little threat."

His English was poor but understandable. He gestured with his rifle for me to step aside so I wouldn't block the view of the street. I moved next to him, my back against the fence.

"What are you going to do with that?" he asked, pointing mockingly at my notebook and pen, which I always carried with me.

"Well," I said thoughtfully, "maybe you know the saying: 'A pen is more powerful than a sword.' And: 'To hold a pen is to be at war.' In other words, controlling a pen is like being in a battle."

"Never heard of it," said the young Boer with a shrug. "But you might be right."

The young man who had lost his brother in the battle on the mountain walked by, carrying drinks for the sentries.

"Sorry for your loss," I said to him.

He shot me a surly look and turned away without a word. I couldn't blame him. This was a war like any other: high-ranking officials decided that ordinary people should fight each other while they remained safe. It was the ordinary people who had to endure the loss and grief caused by conflict. How do you love your enemies when they've just killed your brother— killed him for reasons you don't even fully understand? Killed by people whose names you don't know, who were given unjustifiable orders to take the land where you were born and raised, and who, like you, were caught up in a situation they barely comprehend? It was all so bewildering.

"How did you manage to take us by surprise and overpower us?" I asked the young Boer.

"Did you know we had climbed the mountain?"

He grinned again. "It was easy with those bright colours you're wearing."

"How did you proceed once you realized we could fire down at you?"

The young Boer glanced around at his friends, who stood watch calmly. The prisoners in the street remained idle, seated in the shadows of the barracks. I took out my notebook and began jotting down his words. The young Boer proved to be an engaging storyteller.

"The Brits are on top of the mountain," our lookout post shouted. Instantly, a soldier ran to General Nicolaas Smit. The entire camp sprang into action—rifles were loaded, and ammunition supplies were checked.

"I need fifty volunteers to train their rifles at the top of the mountain," General Smit ordered.

The men volunteered in no time.

"Your task is to shoot any man who raises his head above the rim. Make every shot count because you might not get a second chance. Meanwhile, the rest of you will climb up, covered by fire from the others."

The men nodded, their weather-beaten, sun-tanned faces showing clear determination.

Led by Joachim Ferreira, Fanus Roos, and Danie Malan, the volunteers took cover behind the rocks of the first plateau. After a six-hour climb, they reached the summit of Majuba Hill just before noon. Our men opened fire, and the fifty volunteers surged over the mountain's crest, defeating your army. The rest you already know," he concluded his story.

I looked up from my notebook, momentarily speechless. "I'm struck by the simplicity of your surprise attack," I admitted.

"Hmm, it's just common sense to use your farmer's brain," the boy replied.

I chuckled at his literal translation from Afrikaans to English.

"Thank you for sharing your story," I said.

I said goodbye and continued down the street between the barracks in search of more news. I found no one in leadership willing to speak with me, so I returned to the barracks and settled into a shaded spot to work on my articles. The men around me were visibly bored, loitering aimlessly or sitting in idle conversation. For them, it was just waiting for whatever would happen next. The atmosphere was one of despondency and defeat.

Each day, the relentless sun beat down on the corrugated iron barracks. Once it grew dark, we were confined to the barracks, packed closely together and bored. A few small oil lamps cast a dim light. The barracks still reeked of sweat, blood, and illness. Some soldiers, showing their compassion, attended to the wounded through the night.

"I want out of here," the rebellious Fred complained to Dylan.

My field mat was situated next to Fred's and Dylan's, so I overheard their conversation.

Dylan warned him, "Keep your voice down, man," he hissed. "The Boers might hear you and put you in shackles. At least for now, we can still move around."

Others soon joined the conversation. "Just relax," said a tall, gangly fellow who had a bed at the other side of Fred and Dylan's bed, "the authorities are surely negotiating about us."

"Huh," Fred sneered. "Do you really think they care about us? I'm not going to sit around waiting for those slow bureaucrats to make a decision. No one here controls my life but me."

I found his comment rather ironic, given that he was confined and wasn't allowed to leave the prisoner-of-war camp.

Dylan attempted to reason with Fred but eventually gave up.

Later that evening, I overheard Fred hissing to Dylan, "You'd better come with me."

Fred then turned his gaze toward me when he noticed I was following their conversation, his eyes filled with hostility. "And you," he said, "keep your mouth shut and don't write anything about this."

I stared back at him intensely. He shouldn't think that I was afraid of him. I may not have been a muscular soldier like him, but I was man enough to defend myself.

"It's not wise, Fred," I said calmly.

Fred squinted his eyes into slits. In the dim light of the oil lamps, he looked dark and menacing. I didn't let myself be intimidated, but I braced myself in case he decided to attack me. Fred saw that I was not being manipulated and turned away from me. For minutes, he whispered to Dylan. Unfortunately, I couldn't hear what they were saying, but I didn't expect much good from it.

The lamps were dimmed so that the men who wanted to sleep wouldn't be disturbed by the light. When it grew quiet, Fred and Dylan cautiously got up and slipped out the door into the darkness of the night. Along with the tall, gangly fellow who had also noticed their escape, I waited anxiously to see if the Boer guards would notice the two of them. It remained quiet for a while, and I picked up my pen and scribbled on my writing paper.

Suddenly, shots rang out through the night, followed by a blood-curdling scream. Everyone in the barrack woke up with a start.

"What was that?" was whispered all around.

The tall, gangly fellow and I remained silent. We looked at each other with worried expressions in our eyes. Had we lost two more of our mates? My heart pounded, and I thought of our families and acquaintances in Vancouver. Would they have to live without them?

We heard rapid footsteps running past the barrack and held our breath in suspense. We heard barking.

"They're sending the dogs after them," whispered the tall, gangly fellow.

Another shot rang out, this time from far outside the camp. A dog howled. A new shot was fired from within the camp. There was a scream. We had no idea what had happened or who had been hit by the shots.

The rest of the evening and through the night, the atmosphere in the barrack was tense. I heard men getting up and moving around to use the latrine more often than on other nights. They, like me, probably couldn't sleep.

The next day, we all had to line up on the road between the barracks. Commandant-General Piet Joubert addressed us. I couldn't understand everything he said. Perhaps his English was poor, or maybe it was due to the strong wind whistling past my ears, or perhaps I was simply too far away. What it came down to was that we received a stern warning. Midway through his speech, someone was dragged forward by

22

a Boer. It was Dylan! He limped and leaned on a stick as if something was wrong with his legs.

Joubert pointed at Dylan. "This prisoner attempted to escape. We shot him in the leg. The next person who tries to escape will get a bullet in their head."

He made no mention of Fred. Did he not know they had tried to escape together? Or didn't he want to admit they failed in chasing a prisoner? Maybe I would never know the reason.

Joubert continued his speech, "Peace negotiations are underway between Paul Kruger and Sir Evelyn Wood at Amajuba Hill. Until there is a resolution, whether it be peace or continued war, you will remain here. I advise you to behave if you wish to leave this camp alive."

He turned, and without granting us another look, he walked away.

When we returned to our barrack, we asked Dylan, "Where is Fred?"

He shrugged, and snapped with a face distorted with pain, "I don't know."

I stop reading and look around the circle. Mom has tears in her eyes and dabs them with a white lace handkerchief.

"I told you," Dad says, "they're stuck in a camp."

Rose and Jasmin have their thumbs in their mouths and are leaning against my shoulder as if I've just read them a bedtime story. I don't think they grasp the seriousness of what's in the letter.

"Keep reading," Kate says with a trembling voice. Her face looks pale.

I pick up the letter again and continue reading.

೪೦೪

At the end of March, we received another speech from Joubert. We stood stoically in the space between the barracks, waiting for what he would say. His speech was very brief.

"The peace treaty between the English and the Boers has been signed. We will no longer hold you in this camp. You are free."

A loud cheer broke out. We danced around, hugged each other, and patted each other on the shoulders. Without paying further attention to Joubert and the other Boers, we turned and went into the barracks to pack our things. We were heading to our homes in England or Canada. We had no reason to stay here any longer.

We had a long foot journey in front of us to the coast. Unfortunately, the work on the railway that the Boers, with the help of the Dutch and Germans, were building had been interrupted by the war. So now we were forced to walk. We lined up in a long queue to leave for Port Saint John. Some of the wounded lay on quickly assembled stretchers. Other wounded, like Dylan, had to walk on their own. Dylan's leg was healing poorly and visibly pained him while walking. The men with the stretchers went ahead, followed by the wounded who could walk but needed to lean on other soldiers. The healthy soldiers carried all the equipment that the Boers had allowed us to keep.

Before the last in line left the camp, I went looking for the young Boer who had previously told me the story about the ambush on the mountain. The Boers were also busy packing their belongings.

"I see you're leaving too," I said to the young Boer when I saw him.

"Yes," he said, "it's time to return to our families and pick up the thread of normal life again. Although," he said thoughtfully, "I don't think it will ever be normal again after everything we've been through."

"I think you're right," I said. "Take care. Thanks for treating us well," I said, shaking his hand.

His hand felt like a block of African hardwood in mine.

"All the best," he said.

I joined the end of the line of soldiers that had slowly started moving. Even the last, healthy soldiers looked like a bunch of paupers. A few weeks of captivity can make a huge difference in the appearance of a group of young men.

The sun burned intensely on our heads. We made slow progress. At night, we shivered from the cold and discomfort of lying on the hard ground in the open air in the makeshift camp we set up. After a week of walking, our feet were battered and bloody from the open blisters. We were now close to the coast and Port Saint John, and in the distance, we could see the ocean. When we stood in front of the bridge over the Mzimvubu, the men enthusiastically pointed at the blue water. New energy entered the men's stride as leaving this dry, hot land seemed so close. We crossed the bridge and continued on the cart path that ran along the bay. The end was in sight. The sun blazed, and the sky was a clear blue with a few white clouds. My back was sweaty under my backpack. The remaining kilometres seemed endless. I mechanically placed one foot in front of the other on the dusty road without looking up. My open blisters were painful. Luckily, there were trees and bushes along the path, providing some shade. Then the salty smell of the ocean reached us. A gentle breeze came our way, which was a huge relief, especially for the injured men and those who supported them. Finally, after another two labourious hours, we reached Port Saint John. It was a small settlement of about three hundred people. The village had a few mud huts, some wooden buildings, and a tavern. Most of the inhabitants were European officials, traders, natives, English officers, and soldiers.

We asked at the tavern when the ship that would take us to the Cape and from there to England would arrive. No one could say for sure. So, we spent the following days drinking and mostly waiting.

Each day, I took a walk around the village, looking for an interesting story. I approached the lumberjacks who brought wagons full of wood from the forest to the lumber merchants. The wood was to be shipped to Europe to make durable furniture. These men looked poor but proud, just like the Boers. They looked at me with shy disdain and gave little to no answers to my questions. I could not be sure if they didn't understand me or simply didn't want to talk to me.

Every day, I also walked to the ocean and looked out from between the mountains that blocked much of the view of the ocean, hoping to see a ship approaching. There wasn't much to see or write about, and I looked forward to going to the Cape.

One morning, when we had been in Port Saint John for about a week, a man staggered out of the forest. He was exhausted, and his clothes were torn. At first, I didn't recognize him, but when he opened his mouth and said, "What an irritating bunch of Boers," I realized it was Fred.

"Where have you been?" I asked, surprised.

With a grunt, he replied, "Give me some water; I'm dying of thirst."

I gave him my water bottle. After he drank greedily, a flood of swear words came from his lips that didn't make me any wiser about where he had actually been. I walked with him to the tavern, where the soldiers were staying. I kept within earshot because I wanted to know what had really happened. Bit by bit, I found out. That night of the escape, he had walked through the dark forest. At every sound, he feared it was one of the dogs the Boers had sent after him. No one had followed him; they probably thought Dylan was the only one who had escaped. He had endured a thousand terrors. Every breaking twig could have been an elephant. He pictured himself being crushed by a massive, bulky giant angry at the white people for hunting them for their tusks. Eventually, he climbed a tree and felt somewhat safer. He hadn't slept, and his stomach started growling. At dawn, he continued his way through the almost impenetrable forest until he stumbled upon a hut. The old woman who lived there gave him something to eat. She seemed unaware of what was happening in the world. She directed him south, toward the ocean, after making him do a few days' worth of chores around the hut that were too heavy for her. He eventually made his way to the coast, quite far from the harbour. His hunger was so great that he took the risk of asking a few lumberjacks where he could catch a ship to England. They didn't understand a word he said, but when they took him to another lumberjack who could understand a bit of English, they got what he meant. They directed him to Port Saint John and said it was just a day's walk.

"I don't know how those lumberjacks walk, but it took me three days to get here," Fred grumbled.

He looked bedraggled, probably from hunger, lack of alcohol, and exhaustion.

In hindsight, it had been a waste of time and risk to escape. Only four weeks after his escape, the treaty was signed.

For a moment, I place the letter on my lap.

Sarah pours us an aperitif. "In 15 minutes, I can serve dinner, madame," she says to Mom.

Mom nods absently. I have one more page to read. I can finish it before we sit at the table. Rose, my boisterous little sister, has fallen asleep on my shoulder, and Jasmin's eyes are also drooping. Mom has her cup of lavender chamomile tea tightly clasped in her hands. It seems she hasn't drunk much of it yet.

"Well, well," Dad says, "those boys have been through quite a lot."

"I hope Dylan's leg is healing. I wish they would come home soon so a good doctor can look at it," Kate says.

I turn the last page over and over. When everyone is quiet again, I read on.

I'm writing this last part of the letter while we're on our way to the Cape. At the end of the week, after Fred rejoined our group, the ship arrived.

"You're back just in time, lad," grumbled a soldier stationed in Port Saint John to Fred. Fred grumbled back.

Our belongings were loaded, and now we're sailing to the Cape. At the Cape, I will send my articles about the war and the letter to you by mail. Now I need to decide where I'm going. At least somewhere exciting. Staying in South Africa is not an option now that the peace treaty with the Boers has been signed and calm has returned. I hear everyone talking about the gold discovered in Klondike, in the northwest of Canada.

"Come along, then," Fred said, "gold hunting is much more lucrative than writing articles."

I laughed, but he was probably right. With so many people caught up in the gold rush, there should be plenty to write about. First, Dylan and I will go to Vancouver to visit our families and you. Unfortunately, Fred doesn't see the point in taking such a long detour.

Dylan hasn't finished his letter yet. I'll send mine ahead. I hope to see you soon.

Warm regards,

Paul Oakes

I put the letter on the sideboard. My heart is singing. Paul is coming home soon! Will I be able to persuade him to stay in Vancouver for good? I immediately push that thought out of my mind. Paul loves traveling the world and writing articles about his experiences.

Paul, Dylan, and Fred are only eighteen. They are all very different, but they share a love for adventure. They have known each other since elementary school and have been inseparable.

Kate and I also attended that same school. Kate is fifteen and a year older than I am.

A few years ago, she came to live with us after her parents died of smallpox. Kate works in a sewing workshop, and I am training to become a teacher at the school where the twins also go.

We sit down at the table as Sarah serves the dishes. Dad has this strange habit of reading his newspaper at the table. Even though today we're not talking about ribbons and bows but about our friends coming home, he picks up the Vancouver Weekly Herald out of habit.

"Look," he says, surprised, "here's Paul's article about the war in South Africa."

Dad reads a few excerpts, but we've already received a much more personal account in the letter Paul sent us.

"They'll be arriving in a few weeks, too," Dad says.

The twins, who are wide awake again, clap their hands.

"Are you going to marry Dylan?" Rose asks Kate.

Kate blushes. "Girl, I'm still way too young, and he's never asked me, remember?"

The twins pout.

"First, we need to see how serious his injuries are," Dad says.

"Dad," says Mom, "I didn't expect that from you. Kate can't refuse him just because he was injured in the war. It's actually a sign of bravery."

"Bravery?" Dad says sharply. "I consider it more of a misplaced and thoughtless act."

I have to admit Dad has a point.

"I hope Dylan has learned his lesson and won't listen to Fred so much anymore. Dylan always lets Fred influence him too much."

Kate looks a bit disheartened.

"But," Dad says, looking at Kate, "you have a few more years to think about it and make the right decision. Let's first wait for the arrival of the boys. We'll see what happens later."

Kate nods. She often keeps a bit aloof during table conversations, although we've included her as a family member since she only had us as her direct relatives. Kate and I get along very well. She has always been like an older sister to me. Sometimes I suspect she feels a bit outside the family. Now that Dad has said this, it probably reinforces her feeling of not quite belonging, I think.

"Dear sister," I say later that evening as we're getting ready for bed, and I'm brushing Kate's hair, "you shouldn't take what Dad said to heart. He means well."

"I know," says Kate, "but I'm not his real daughter."

"Kate," I say reprimandingly, "he treats you as his real daughter and tries to give you good advice. Besides, I see you as my real sister."

I lean forward and lay my cheek against hers. As I continue brushing her hair, I see tears glistening in her eyes in the mirror.

"Thank you," Kate whispers.

"Kate, Dylan's letter has arrived!"

Rose dances into the living room, followed closely by Jasmin. Rose's long skirts and blonde hair are dancing with her movements.

Kate looks up from her sewing, surprised, and reaches for the letter.

Rose drops the letter into her hand. "Read it out loud, will you?" she asks excitedly. "Open it, I want to know what it says."

"Calm down," says Jasmin, who stands behind Rose and looks over her shoulder.

Kate turns the letter around and around.

"The stamp on the letter is from Halifax," she says. Her face lights up. "It was posted in Canada. The boys are back in Canada!" she exclaims joyfully.

She starts nervously laughing, and Rose begins dancing again. "Open the letter now," she says anxiously. "Read what it says."

I sit in the chair opposite Kate, watching the whole situation unfold. I can't help but smile at the enthusiasm with which Rose experiences the world. She's always the more daring one of the twins. Jasmin is much more cautious and thoughtful. She thinks before she acts but is almost always persuaded to join in on Rose's wild ideas.

"Is Dylan going to ask you to marry him? Does it say that in the letter?" Rose asks.

Kate laughs. "Don't be silly," and then more seriously, "He's just come back from a war. They lost the war, and above that, he's injured. His mind probably isn't on proposing. Besides, we're still way too young. Can you please pass me the letter opener?"

Rose immediately turns around and bumps into Jasmin. "Why are you standing so close behind me?" she says.

Jasmin shrugs and sits on the edge of Kate's armchair while Rose looks for the letter opener. Rose hands it to Kate, who tears open the letter. Her eyes scan over the lines.

"What does it say?" Rose asks impatiently.

Kate reads silently. She turns the paper over. The back is also written on. Jasmin follows along as best she can.

"Let me have a look too. Move over," says Rose, pushing against Jasmin.

"Don't," says Jasmin as she tries to continue reading.

Rose sits on her sister's lap, but that's too much for Jasmin. She pushes Rose off her lap, and as Rose grabs Jasmin, they both slide off the ground with a thud.

Then, Mom comes into the room. "What's all this noise?" she asks, immediately noticing the twins flailing on the floor.

"Mom," Rose calls, "Kate has a letter from Dylan, and she won't read it out loud."

Mom's interest is piqued. "How is he?" she asks Kate.

"As we know, Dylan was shot in the leg by the Boers. It still bothers him quite a bit," Kate says.

"Does he have to have his leg amputated?" Rose asks immediately. "How awful of those Boers."

"Be quiet now, girl," Mom says nervously and irritated, "let Kate tell us."

Kate reads parts of the letter.

"The boys are in Canada and hope to arrive in British Columbia by train this week. From there, they will continue by stagecoach. They expect to arrive in Vancouver on Saturday."

There is a moment of silence, and then I say, "It's Friday today, so they'll be arriving tomorrow."

The twins start dancing again. "Can the boys come here?" the girls ask Mom.

Mom nods. "They can come here for dinner on Sunday if Paul's grandmother and Dylan's parents agree."

I stand up. "My lunch break is over. I'm going back to school."

"See you tonight," they all call as I close the door behind me.

This afternoon is the last of the school year. As the teacher's assistant, it's my job to read aloud for half an hour at the end of the day while Miss Jones corrects the final dictations. Reading aloud is also the only thing that keeps the children calm in the sweltering classroom. The windows are all wide open opposite each other. The gentle breeze from the harbour doesn't offer much relief. The children are looking forward to the summer vacation.

I'm also happy about the upcoming free days. I look forward to working in the vegetable garden with the herbs, from which I make tinctures. Ma will be glad too. She hasn't had much help from the twins, who play more than they do chores. Kate is only home at lunchtime. She works long hours at the sewing workshop. When she finished school, she insisted on learning a skill to support herself if necessary. Pa and Ma were hesitant but agreed. Kate has, after all, an inheritance from her parents that would more than support her.

I also wanted to learn a trade, and being a teacher seemed like a suitable choice. The school where Kate and I attended and where I now work is funded by the church we belong to. The pastor put in a good word for me with the headmaster, so I ended up in Miss Jones's class to gain practical experience.

Finally, the last school bell of the year rings. The summer vacation has begun. The children bounce up from their seats. I stand next to Miss Jones by the door and shake hands with the children. We wish them all God's blessings and a good vacation. Billy is the last. He hesitates and gives me a somewhat unwilling handshake.

"Have a nice vacation, Bill," I say.

He shrugs. "I'd rather be at school," he says stiffly.

I understand. Billy has to work hard on his parents' farm during the summer months. I hold his hand for a moment. "You know," I say, "the library is open every Friday evening. Ask your parents if you can come and borrow a book, then you can enjoy reading on Sundays."

He nods, and his face looks a bit happier. "I'll ask my pa," he says.

Then he, too, runs out the door. Free from school, but not free from work.

The next afternoon, Kate and I, along with the twins, head to the stop at Joseph Mannion's Inn at the intersection of Kingsway and Gladstone Street to see if the stagecoach is approaching. Along the busy street, we keep the girls by our hands. They skip along with us while the horses and trams thunder by, stirring up dust on the dry streets. The stagecoach isn't here yet, so we pass the time by looking at shop windows.

"Look, look," Rose suddenly exclaims excitedly, "the stagecoach is coming!"

Indeed, in the distance, a coach is approaching at high speed down the main street. Six horses are pulling the coach. Panting and sweating, they stop in front of the inn. Men who have made the trip on the roof jump to the ground. Other passengers disembark from the coach one by one. Suitcases that were tied on top and behind are unloaded. The horses are unharnessed, and fresh horses are hitched in their place.

"Paul!" the twins cheer. "There's Paul!"

Paul has jumped off the roof and is walking toward the coach's step. Then Dylan emerges. He struggles to get down the steps, and Paul offers him a helping hand. They gather their suitcases, and then they spot us. We are greeted with enthusiasm.

"Hey, how nice!" says Paul, and Dylan also has a joyful grin on his face. "We didn't know you were coming to pick us up."

"Surprise," Rose shouts, and the twins make a few happy jumps.

Paul lifts the girls one by one, twirls them around, and then comes to me. He tries to shake the twins off, but they cling to his arms. He laughs.

"I'm glad you're back," I say.

"So am I," he replies simply.

Then his attention is immediately grabbed again by the twins, who are hanging onto his sleeves. Dylan greets Kate, and she smiles shyly at him.

On the way home, we can see just how badly Dylan is limping.

"Shall we take a tram?" I suggest.

"No," Dylan grumbles, "my leg is just a bit stiff from sitting in the coach for so long. Movement is good for me."

So, we continue walking, adjusting to Dylan's pace. He hadn't written much about it, but the chance that he will be limited in his daily activities seems high.

Will it be a good choice for Kate to marry him? Well, she still has at least three years to think about it. The twins bombard

Dylan with questions about how he got the wound in his leg. He evades the questions and gives vague answers. I can imagine the young men have nightmares about the war and don't always want to be reminded of the violent events.

We approach the intersection where our paths diverge. Paul goes to his grandmother's, and Dylan to his parents and siblings.

"You're invited to come to lunch with us tomorrow after church," Kate says.

"Yippee," the twins cheer, "then you can tell us all about your adventures."

Kate and I look apologetically at the young men, shrugging as if we can't help that the twins talk so much. But actually, we are just as eager to hear all the stories.

The next day after church, Dylan and Paul receive a warm welcome from my parents. My father especially wants to know every detail about the war in Africa. The faces of the women are full of sympathy for all the victims of the war. Ma gives Dylan some of the arnica and calendula salve I made from the plants in our herb garden to apply to his leg wound.

"Tell us about the sea voyage back to Canada," Pa encourages Paul to talk.

That journey isn't really worth talking about," Paul begins. "I felt seasick for days. Finally, it eased a bit, and I got my sea legs—or at least regained my balance—so I didn't feel so sick anymore. Until a big storm came, and I was seasick again. The sailors laughed about it, saying the storm was nothing special.

First, we went to England, and from there, we sailed to Halifax. The overland journey west was mostly by train. There's quite a story about that too." Paul looks at us. "I was sitting next to a Chinese man on the train who told me about it. He was hard to understand like all Asians trying to speak English, but by patiently listening, I managed to get the gist of it."

Pa's eyes are questioning. "Tell us," he says.

I suspect Pa is just as curious as Paul, but while Paul writes down everything, so others can read it, Pa just consumes all the available information.

"The train tracks, as far as they are completed, are being laid under the supervision of William van Horne and road builder Andrew Onderdonk. These two men brought thousands of Chinese workers from China and California as cheap labor. The Chinese are paid in rice mats, so they can't buy extra food, leading to many deaths from scurvy. They also have the dangerous task of blasting rocks with the unreliable explosive nitroglycerin. Because of that, many Chinese workers die, and as an alternative, they choose to try their luck on the goldfields."

"How sad," Pa concludes.

"We could only go as far as the Rockies by freight train; then we had to continue by stagecoach. And now we're back home," Paul finishes his story.

"And," Pa asks Dylan, "what are your plans for your future?"

"I don't have many plans, Mr. Hawthorne, as long as my leg troubles me. Miss Jones said this morning after the service that they're looking for someone at the prospectors' store. I'll go visit there tomorrow to see if they can use me."

"Good idea," says Pa. "Gold prospecting will probably continue for a while. Gold seekers need a lot of supplies. I hope you get the job. And you, Paul, do you already have a new assignment from your boss?"

"I'm going to visit the office tomorrow to propose writing an article about Klondike. I'd like to go there and see what it's like to live and work in a gold mining camp."

"Are you going to look for gold?" Rose immediately jumps onto Paul's lap. "Will you get rich?"

"Certainly," Paul says with a laugh, "I plan to get stinking rich."

He winks at me. I feel a blush rise, but fortunately, no one is looking at me, and all attention is focused on Rose and Paul.

Dylan has gotten the job at the prospectors' store, and Paul has actually received permission to go to Klondike to write about life as a gold miner.

"I'll write to you," Paul promises while we are alone in the kitchen on the last evening before he leaves and is saying his goodbyes. I feel sad, and it's clearly written on my face.

"I'm not leaving the earth," he adds comfortingly. It doesn't help much.

Thankfully, he keeps his word. After a few weeks, a letter arrives addressed to "Elsa and family."

"Hey," says Jasmin, who reads the address with me as I open the letter. "Why did he write your name on top?"

She looks at me questioningly, and I blush. I shrug. Out of the corner of my eye, I see Kate smiling at us, but luckily, she says nothing.

"You're his girlfriend, aren't you?" Jasmin teases.

"Read it after dinner," Dad says. "I'm also curious about what he has to report from the far north. The temperatures over there must be dropping by now. I wonder if he'll stay there for the winter with all the heavy snow, they always get there."

After dinner, we all sit in the living room, and I begin to read:

❧

Dear Elsa and family,

After the experiences in the Boer War, I have now found myself in a very different situation. In the war, soldiers relied on each other as comrades and worked as a team as much as possible. Here, everyone is focused on themselves. There is an atmosphere of distrust and envy. It is difficult to gain the trust of the prospectors and to find information for my stories. Let me start at the beginning.

With the money I earned from my articles about the Boer War, I wanted to buy a permit for a piece of land where I could search for gold. At the office in Dawson Creek, in the north of British Columbia, near the border with Alaska, where the permits were issued, was a long line of men, all with the same goal in mind. They all wanted to get rich quickly. Inch by inch, the line shuffled forward. Eventually, this line would come to an end, and I would be able to go to the piece of land where I was allowed to search for gold. Finally, it was my turn, and I received my permit.

I set out for the goldfields after first buying a gold pan, a pickaxe, and a shovel. I already had a tent, cooking, and drinking utensils. I was also advised that food was so expensive and scarce in the gold miners' camp that I should stock up on a good supply in Skagway before heading into the mountains. After that, I only had to follow the long line of men who climbed up and down the mountains to bring their supplies to where the gold was found. It's an advantage that I have Canadian nationality. Men and women coming from America are required to bring enough food to survive a year. Still, I had trouble hauling everything I had bought. My shoulders hurt from the straps of my backpack digging into my skin. The bags I carried in my hands cut into my palms too.

The journey seemed endless, but, as with everything, it eventually came to an end. With the permit in hand, I arrived at the prospectors' camp. It was complete chaos. Fortune-seeking men and also women were standing in front of the mining office, showing their papers. Their belongings were scattered everywhere while they stood in line for the office. There was an atmosphere of great anticipation. Fortunately, the line for the office was not as long as in Dawson Creek. A cool breeze felt wonderful after the strenuous climb with all the gear I carried. The official pointed me in the direction of my purchased land. I picked up my things and set out to cover the last part of the journey to my gold mining experience.

I found the stakes marking my claim and let the tools slide off my back. First, I set up my tent and searched for some firewood to cook a meal. As best as I could, I made a cup of tea and baked some of the outrageously expensive vegetables and meat I had bought in Skagway.

And you won't believe this, but later that evening, when it started to get dark, and I was still outside by the fire, my neighbour staggered drunkenly onto the piece of land next to mine. You probably guessed it—

it was Fred. Although he is my school friend, comrade in arms, and now my neighbour, I still plan to stay a bit away from him.

Fred was too drunk to recognize me, and I soon heard him snoring in his tent. When he had slept off his drunkenness, he was as surprised as I was that we had become neighbours.

Fred went panning for gold, and I took my notebook and pen and went out to explore. I planned to describe my first impressions of the miners' camp. Later, I would go search for gold.

The sun had just risen, but the village was already bustling with activity. Newly arrived gold miners climbed the path to the village to take possession of their purchased plots. Several miners were going down the mountain.

I approached one of those men. "Are you leaving already?" I asked interestedly.

The man shook his head. "No, we have more supplies down below that need to be hauled up. We are a group of men, and we take turns going down until everything is brought up the mountain. After that, the last man can come up as well, and we can set up the gold troughs. We have plots of land that border a mountain stream. We will make good use of the water to wash the gold." He tipped his cowboy hat. "I'm off. There's still a lot to do before winter sets in."

I went in search of a story. I avoided the house of ill repute, even though someone literally grabbed my jacket. "Hey, handsome," said an elaborately dressed lady.

I pulled away and walked to the pub, the ultimate place for Wild West stories. I ordered a beer, and although I didn't want to waste my money there, I saw it as an investment to get to know the bartender. It was still early in the morning, and the bar was empty except for a few drunkards. I spoke to the bartender and asked how things were going in the gold miners' village.

"Very well for me," he said, laughing, and his large belly shook.

Then he became more serious. "Not everyone is doing so well here," he said, nodding toward the few men who were drunk as a skunk lying over their tables.

"Some people can't handle wealth and waste all their money. Every penny they find in gold, they bring here."

"Where do you exchange gold for money?" I asked. "Is there a bank here?"

"No, for that, you have to go to Dawson Creek," said the bartender.

We exchanged some more information, and the bartender promised to keep his eyes and ears open for news that might be of interest to me. I thanked him and went to try to make small talk with the grocer, but he was way too busy.

When I have more news, I will write to you again.

Warm regards,

Paul Oaks

I put the letter back in the envelope and place it on the coffee table.

"I wonder how long he'll manage there," says Dad. "That he ended up right next to Fred! I hope he won't spend too much time with him."

That evening, while lying in bed, I keep thinking about the letter, not so much worried about whether Paul will spend time with Fred, but more about the fact that there are so many women in a mining camp seeking men's attention. I try to push away the troubling thought.

I pray to God, asking Him to keep Paul on the right path since I see no way of doing it myself.

Later in the fall, another letter from Paul arrives. Dylan is visiting us when I read it out loud.

"You should be glad you're here in Vancouver," Mom says to him. "I can't imagine being in that high, cold north, with hardly any comforts and no luxuries."

Dylan says nothing but stares blankly ahead. I can imagine that a young man like him would prefer having no luxury over limping and always being in pain. Every day, he is reminded of his failed, useless escape attempt.

I open the letter, and when everyone is seated around the hearth, I begin to read.

Dear Elsa and family,

The conversation that morning with the miner, who was heading down the mountain to fetch more supplies and buy some of the extremely expensive food from the village store, got me thinking. I needed to divide my time between searching for gold, building a cabin, and stocking up on food for the winter. On top of all that, I should be working on my articles.

I searched for wood for a log cabin and spent every day panning for gold in the river. The river got colder by the day as the days shortened and autumn approached. I fished in the river, dried the fish, gathered wild plants and berries, and dried everything in the sun or over the campfire.

My plot of land is along the river, and every day I sift for gold for hours. Some days I find nothing; other days are better. I don't find much, but I collect it diligently without telling anyone or wasting it. My gold stash grows slowly.

I did well to make a plan for the winter. With the First Nations who regularly come to the village to trade, I exchanged gold for reindeer hides. I used these to line the inside of my small log cabin. I also stockpiled a large amount of firewood for the stove. It makes the space inside quite cramped, but I don't want to risk it being stolen. The mentality of the gold miners is miserable. Most of the men are okay, but there are a few con artists who try to trick newcomers into entrusting them with a portion of their money or to cheat them out of all their money through card games.

Once a week, I eat at Violet's restaurant. Violet is a nice, cheerful woman of about thirty and cooks delicious meals. The men pay her with gold nuggets. I suspect she is one of the wealthiest villagers. I always sit at someone's table in search of stories. Most men don't tell me much, afraid that someone will know how much gold they have. Some tell me all sorts of things about home, their families, girlfriends, and children they miss.

Some gold miners don't look very strong. They have no beards, no rough hands, and they have soft voices. More and more of these miners grouped together until it became clear to me that they were women in men's clothing also looking for gold. They bring a sense of home but keep as much distance as possible from the men and stick together. I can't blame them. Life in the camp is harsh and rough.

I noticed how few gold miners thought ahead. Were they not aware of the fierce cold and the snow that would come in winter? I understood that those from warmer regions who have no experience with the cold in Alaska and northern British Columbia were unprepared for the harsh winter.

Fred is a good example of living day by day. He has more luck with finding gold than others, but he sits from sunrise to sunset, sifting in the river.

However, he spends what he finds in the pub, on frivolous women, and gambling. I understand that he is trying to drown out his traumatic experiences from South Africa, but his drinking has turned into an addiction that keeps getting worse.

Already early in the fall, the first snow had fallen, and the layer gets thicker as time goes on. It is no fun standing in the river with half-frozen hands and feet, shaking my pan of dirt. I have to get out of the water every five minutes to warm myself by the fire. Every day, I tell myself I can't go on like this. Every day I consider leaving. Then I hear about someone who has struck a gold vein, and I keep going.

"I'm going back to Vancouver," I shouted one December morning to Fred, who was standing in the river a little farther down. It was snowing, and the sky was grey.

"Have you gone mad?" Fred shouted back. "How do you think you'll get there in this weather?"

I knew he was right. To undertake the journey in this weather is more madness than staying here in the cold. As long as the river flows, there's a chance that gold will come by. So, I stayed. I am sometimes hungry, I am freezing, but I have decided to stubbornly hold out until spring.

Warm regards,

Paul Oaks

"Good grief, boy," Mom sighs as I put down the letter. "What are you doing to yourself?"

She puts into words what we all think but don't say out loud.

"This time, I agree with Fred," Dad states soberly. "Paul has no choice but to stay there until the snow melts."

The winter months in Vancouver are wet, cold, and grey. Often, thick clouds hang over the city for days, and it rains constantly. The mood of the city's inhabitants drops to zero. People rush through the streets without acknowledging each other. In the shops, people grumble about the weather and shiver from the damp cold while waiting their turn. The rain, which turns the streets into muddy puddles, gives Sarah a lot of extra work. The bottoms of our skirts are dirty and wet from the mud after every walk to work and the shops. A pleasant walk in the park is out of the question with this weather. Fortunately, the children in the class I co-teach with Miss Jones don't let the weather bother them much. Sometimes it snows for a few days, which is great fun for the children, but, for me, it makes me think of the far north where Paul is. I worry. It's been so long since we heard from him. Even the mail apparently cannot reach us from Klondike.

Until one day, early in the spring, a letter finds its way to Vancouver, to our home. I can hardly wait for everyone to sit down that evening so I can read it to them.

Dear Elsa and family,

I know it's already nice weather in Vancouver. Here, it takes such an extremely long time for the sun to come far enough north to make it a bit warmer and to get us out of our isolation.

Finally, we can send mail through the courier again. I hope this letter finds you in good health.

I've earned back the money I invested in this whole venture. For me, it's time to return to Vancouver.

There's not much more to write about here, other than crime and fraud. That's why the Vancouver Weekly Herald only got a few stories from me.

I've sold my piece of land to Fred. He must have pulled quite a lot from the river because even with his extravagant spending, he still had enough to pay me, which he did without complaint.

Fred couldn't resist accusing me of abandoning him. "You're not a real man," he had to add. Still, I send you his regards. So, here they are...

I'm sending this letter ahead; I'll be taking the next mail coach. I'm going to pack my things and say goodbye to Fred, the innkeeper, and Violet. I haven't made many other friends.

My letter should reach you a week before I arrive in Vancouver.

Best regards,

Paul Oaks

"Thank goodness," Mom sighs. "He's coming home. How happy his grandmother will be. Every Sunday, she asks if we've heard anything. She'll probably have received a letter herself by now."

"I'll go by her place later," Dad says, "to make sure she's received a message as well."

I feel nervously elated. Paul is on his way to Vancouver!

"What are you primping yourself up for?" Kate teases as I stand in front of the mirror on Sunday morning before church, paying extra attention to my appearance. "Expecting someone?"

I stick my tongue out at her.

Kate laughs. "I hope he arrived yesterday."

"I hope so, too," I say nervously.

We arrive at church a little early, and my eyes keep drifting to the place where Paul's grandmother always sits.

Suddenly, Kate nudges me. "He's here," she whispers.

I turn my head and see Paul walking into the church behind his grandmother.

He looks in our direction and gives me a smiling nod. I would love to dance and jump like the twins always do when they're happy about something, but I behave like a proper young lady and smile and nod back. After the service, of which, to my embarrassment, I remember little, Mom invites Paul and his grandmother to lunch at our home. Paul offers me his arm, and we chat cheerfully as we walk the short distance home. Behind us walk Kate and Dylan. Mom has given Grandma an arm, and the twins are dancing, holding Dad's hands.

While enjoying a cup of tea and a ginger cookie, we listen to Paul's stories.

"In Vancouver, the temperature was so pleasant when I arrived that I almost regretted my decision to leave Klondike. Then I remembered the cold and hunger of the past winter. And, of course, I wanted to see Grandma and all of you again. After visiting Grandma yesterday, I went by the newspaper office. I immediately got an assignment to interview a former gold miner. The maid at the large, wealthy house where I knocked on the door, let me in and showed me to a seat in the reception room. To my surprise, a man walked in whom I recognized as one of the gold miners from Klondike. We had sat at the same table at Violet's restaurant. He looked very shabby back then, just like all of us. We chatted a bit back and forth, without him revealing much about what he had found, which didn't surprise me. He told me he was done with gold mining.

"Is this," I asked him, gesturing with a wide sweep of my arm at the beautiful things in the large room with the high ceiling, "what you meant when you said you were done with gold mining?"

The man laughed heartily. "Yes, indeed. It was just too dangerous to let anyone know that I had found so much.

Now everything is safely invested in this house, and the rest is in the bank."

We talked about his time in the gold miners' camp, and he let me write down a few interesting tidbits for my article."

Everyone is hanging on Paul's every word.

After tea, Kate and I go to the kitchen to prepare lunch. Sarah always spends Sundays with her parents and siblings.

"Stay and enjoy yourself with Grandma," Kate tells Mom, gently pushing her back into the chair she's about to get up from.

In the kitchen, we heat the soup and slice the bread. We place slices of meat and cheese on a glass platter.

"Are you happy that Paul is back?" Kate asks.

I nod. "I hope he stays in Vancouver a bit longer. I don't like that he always leaves so soon."

"Ask him if he can work at the newspaper office," Kate suggests.

"I don't know if I should do that. He needs to make his own decisions, and I don't want to influence them. He wants to see the world, which I can certainly understand. I don't want to hold him back from chasing his dreams. He needs to decide for himself whether he wants to stay here; otherwise, he'll definitely get restless and want to leave eventually. Or worse, he'll stay here and become an irritable, unbearable person."

"You're right. You don't have to pin him down just yet. There will surely come a time when he has seen everything and realizes that home is the best place."

"I hope so," I say with a sigh. "I just wonder how long it will take. A year, maybe two?"

Then the twins come running into the kitchen.

"Calm down," I say, handing them plates and cutlery. "Go set the table."

Very carefully, they return to the living room. Kate and I carry the bowls with soup and other food. Soon, we're all seated around the table. Dad leads in prayer, thanking God for Paul's safe return. Secretly, I peek through my eyelashes at the other side of the table. I'm guiltily startled when I notice that Paul's looking back in the same way. I squeeze my eyes shut and only open them again when Dad says, "Amen." My eyes innocently slide over the people around the table and settle back on Paul. He winks. To hide my shyness, I quickly hand Grandma's plate to Mom, who has gotten up to serve the soup.

"Thank you, dear," Grandma nods at me.

As Mom serves the others, Grandma leans toward me and whispers while nodding at Paul, "Can't you persuade him to stay in Vancouver?"

I smile. "I'll do my best," I whisper conspiratorially back.

Paul frowns as if he wants to know what our conversation is about. I give him a somewhat daring smile. I won't reveal my little secret with Grandma to him. Hopefully, one of us can convince him to stay.

In the coming weeks, Paul often picks me up from school in the late afternoon.

"Shall we take a stroll by the harbour?" he asks.

Rain or shine, I always say yes. We walk arm in arm through the busy streets to the calm harbour, where the boats gently rock in the water. Paul enthusiastically talks about the people he has met and the stories he writes about them while we walk along the moored boats. It's even cozier when it rains because then we huddle close together under the umbrella. Unfortunately, Paul's stay in Vancouver comes to an end when he gets an assignment from his boss to head east to cover the elections.

"Come back soon," I say when he tells me the news.

"I will," Paul says with a carefree smile on his face.

The following weeks lack sparkle. The letters Paul sends me weekly somewhat make up for his absence, but nothing compares to his presence.

Spring turns into summer, and the sun shines exuberantly over the city. There are no more raindrops or gloomy clouds that made the past winter so grey. On the first day of summer vacation, I help Mom and Sarah air the beds. In the afternoon, I work in the garden. The ground is hard from the weeks of drought, and it's difficult to get the unwanted plants out of the soil. When I think I've weeded enough, I grab a basket and pick herbs from the garden. I'll make tinctures from the edible and medicinal herbs.

"Good morning," a familiar voice suddenly sounds behind me.

I turn around, surprised. "Paul!" I exclaim. "What a surprise. You're back."

"Sorry, I didn't write to let you know I was coming. I wasn't quite sure what the plan was myself, but," he adds, "I'm here." He spreads his arms, and naturally, I lean into him. We hold each other tightly for a moment. Then the back door opens. Sarah calls to say that the coffee is ready.

The week of walks by the harbour and through the city passes far too quickly. Paul has an assignment in America waiting for him.

Soon, the new school year with a class of new students occupies my mind and diverts my thoughts. I live for Paul's letters, which arrive regularly.

It's Christmas when he suddenly appears in front of me.

"You could have given some notice," I say, a bit irritated.

"I thought you'd like such surprises," Paul jokes.

"Of course, I'm happy to see you again, but you're catching me off guard," I complain.

During one of our long walks, I dare to ask him the question that has been on my mind for so long. "Have you ever seriously considered staying in Vancouver and doing your work here?"

I wait anxiously for an answer. It takes a moment, and then he says, "I feel much too young to settle down in Vancouver for good. I haven't seen everything in the world yet, and now that I have the chance, I'd like to take advantage of it."

It feels like a slap in the face. I try not to show my despair, but Paul senses perfectly that my mood has changed.

"Can't you come with me?" he asks.

I shake my head. "I don't think I can be away from my family for months."

"You can be away from me for months?" Paul asks with a smile, looking at me intently.

"No, not that either," I burst out, tears welling up in my eyes. "What can I do?" I add desperately.

He pulls me into his arms. "I'm always writing to you, right?" he says soothingly.

"That's not the same," I can barely manage to say.

Christmas and the New Year have gotten a dark shadow over them. I feel lost now that the prospect of a future together seems to be fading. I don't know how to handle it.

"Cheer up," Kate says when I tell her. "There will surely come a day when he realizes that the life of a wanderer isn't all that great."

I shrug. "I don't know anymore," I say sadly.

Still, I keep hoping, each time he comes home, that he has changed his mind.

෨෬

"He asked me!" Kate says excitedly as she sits down in her chair.

We're gathered around the dining table waiting for Sarah, who will serve the meal from our finest dishes. The twins bounce up and down with enthusiasm. Mom stands up and embraces Kate in a warm hug. Dad smiles.

Kate's announcement doesn't surprise me. I saw last week that Dad invited Dylan into his office for a talk. They usually stay in the living room if they have something to discuss. I immediately suspected that they had something very confidential to discuss and could only think that Dylan was asking Dad for permission to marry Kate. Now that Dylan has had a stable job at the prospectors' store for years, there's no barrier to starting a family. Dylan still limps but seems to have adjusted to his fate.

Dylan and Kate buy a small house not far from Mom and Dad. I help Kate with the decorating, making their new home as cozy as possible. Meanwhile, Kate works diligently on her linen trousseau, embroidering her new initials on each piece.

The wedding is held at our home on a beautiful summer day. I've done my best to make the garden look pristine. The lavender blooms exuberantly with its soft purple flowers. The combination of grey-green sage and thyme, dark red columbines, red roses, and blue-white violets makes it all the more festive. Mom, with the help of Sarah and the twins, has baked a beautiful cake decorated with lavender, violets, and rose petals. I've added extra flavour to the honey for the tea with lavender and roses.

For weeks, we've been sewing Kate's wedding dress and our attire. Even Rose and Jasmin, though only ten years old, wanted to help. Jasmin has corrected many mistakes made by the impatient Rose, and now that I see them in their beautiful dresses, I'm proud of both of them.

We're all nervous as the first guests arrive. While enjoying a cup of coffee and a chocolate cookie, we wait until all the invited guests are present.

Outside in the garden, we've set up enough chairs so that guests can sit in the shade of the large maple tree during the wedding ceremony.

The minister blesses Kate and Dylan's marriage. "Till death do us part," Dylan and Kate repeat after him, pledging their loyalty to each other. Then it's time to cut the wedding cake. Kate and Dylan are given a large knife, and together they cut a piece from the cake. Sarah and I take over and serve everyone a delicious slice.

"You've outdone yourselves," praises Paul, who is also present.

"Thank you," Sarah and I say in unison.

The beautiful cake we worked so hard on quickly disappears, leaving only a small pile of whipped cream with a few flowers.

"Alright, youngsters," says the minister, who joins us, "Another wedding next year?" and he winks at Paul.

For a moment, I see an uncomfortable dismay in Paul's eyes, but then he laughs and says, "No, no, not so soon, pastor. I still have a lot of traveling and writing to do. A wedding will have to wait."

I feel a wave of sadness come over me. I'm already eighteen and have been waiting for such a long time for Paul to decide to stay at home more in Vancouver. It seems that it won't happen for the foreseeable future. The sunny day has taken on a gloomy shadow that I can't shake off.

When Kate and Dylan leave for their new home at the end of the day, and the guests have departed, the house feels eerily empty. Mom and Dad, the twins, and I relax in the evening outside, recovering from the busy but festive day. We chat and try to process all the lasting impressions of the day.

Then the day arrives when the twins graduate to my class. This is also my first year having my own class, without Ms. Jones's guidance. Everyone is excited in their own way. Mom is worried that the girls will cause me trouble while I brace myself. How will Rose and Jasmin react to having their sister at the front of their classroom? They themselves are thrilled about the fact that I'm going to be their teacher.

Over the past year, I've tried to prepare myself. I need to behave like an adult, and when I sometimes feel exuberant and want to dance with the girls, I try to temper that so it won't be too big of a transition for all three of us. Lately, I've forced myself to be more serious, not just at school where I already was, but also at home. However, I did allow myself to laugh heartily at the funny pranks the girls pulled. Right after that, I would warn them that such things won't be allowed in my class.

Kate says everything will be fine, and Dad says I can handle it. The girls themselves sometimes stick their tongues out at me when I address them about something, and Rose says they'll just do what they want.

The first day of school goes remarkably smoothly. Everything is still new for the students and me. There is quite a bit of fidgeting in the class, which is always the case the first week after summer vacation, as the children need to get used to the school routine again.

"So," Mom asks when I come home with the girls in tow, "how was today?"

"Everything went great," I say.

Rose and Jasmin have also come into the living room. I see them exchanging glances with each other. For a moment, I feel a pang of panic. I feel the pressure in my head from the past day intensify. What mischievous plans are those girls hatching?

"And, girls," Mom asks, "how was your day?"

"Boring," says Rose.

"Okay," says Jasmin.

They sit down at the table, where Sarah pours us a cup of tea.

"What was so boring?" Mom asks Rose.

"Just, we had to sit in a chair all day," she says with a grumpy face. "Can't it be any different?" She looks at me dissatisfied.

I shrug. "That's how it is at school," I say. "Order is necessary to be able to learn."

"Well," Rose says angrily, jumping up, "you'd better change that. I'm not going to school anymore if it stays this boring." Mom also stands up, shocked by Rose's outburst.

From that day on, Rose's rebellious attitude doesn't leave her. In class, she has a face like a storm cloud. She kicks the chair of the boy in front of her or pulls his hair. When I give her a spot in the front row, she spends half the day turned around in her chair. I feel a growing frustration with her behaviour, and the days drag on. Every time I turn to the board to write something, I have to watch for notes being passed around the class. Even during recess, I'm alert when the children play in the yard while I prepare my lessons or grade their lessons in their notebooks. Quite often, someone comes into the classroom crying, accompanied by an angry teacher because my dear sister has pushed someone again. Desperate, I decide to move her desk next to mine. Then pens, pencils, and sheets mysteriously disappear, and I have to keep an eye on that too. I talk to Dad and ask if he could have a word with her. It seems to get better for a while, but soon we're back to square one.

On a fall morning, the class is very restless. I attribute it to the stormy weather. The wind is slamming the rain against the windows, and the sun is nowhere to be seen. It's grey and dark outside. Still, I notice that there is something more distracting the children. There are suppressed giggles, laughter behind hands, and to my horror, I see various glances directed at Rose. What could be going on now? I wonder.

"Boys and girls, take out your math notebooks from your desks," I instruct.

The children dive into the drawer under their desks and pull out their notebooks. I pay special attention to Rose, who takes longer than usual to find her things. I stand next to her desk. She startles, and suddenly something jumps to the ground and runs away. Within seconds, there is a lot of screaming in the class. The girls jump on their chairs, and the boys stand nervously wobbling next to their desks. Rose has jumped out of her seat and is crawling on her hands and knees under the desks. Taken aback, I'm at a loss for words. "Catch it, catch it," the children shout.

A few of the wildest boys join Rose in her chase, crawling between the desks on the floor.

"Thom has it," Bev yells, and she falls off her chair in her excitement.

A lot of nervous laughter follows. Thom carefully hands the animal to Rose.

"Rose, come here," I say sternly.

Slowly, Rose comes toward me, her hands tightly clasped together with something in the bowl of her hands that must not escape again.

"What do you have in your hands?" I ask.

"Look," says Rose guilelessly, holding her hands up as if she's showing me a secret I should be excited about. Doesn't that child understand that I'm at my wits' end with her? I look at her hands, and between her slightly open fingers, I see the snout of a mouse.

"What made you think it was okay to bring this animal into the class?" I ask her, annoyed.

She looks at me, and for a moment, I see something innocent and childlike in her eyes. Then she says, looking at the windows against which the wind and rain are pounding: "It was so wet outside," as if that explains everything.

I shake my head and say, "No, Rose, you know that animals belong outside, rain or no rain. They can handle it; you know that well. You're going to put that animal outside in the school garden now and come back immediately. Do you hear me?"

Rose nods. "Can Jasmin come too?" she dares to ask.

"No," I say firmly, "Jasmin can't come."

That settles it. Rose goes outside with the mouse, and I try to restore order in the class. As soon as everyone is seated again, Rose returns, and the giggling starts up again.

"The mouse is outside?" I ask her just to be sure.

She nods, but from the look in her eyes, I can see she's not telling the whole truth. I give her a stern look. Suddenly, her attitude changes, and she looks at me defiantly.

"Sit down," I command her sternly. I resolve to keep a close watch on her today.

I'm relieved when the bell rings. After finishing the grading, I walk to the headmaster's office, where he is still busy, say goodbye, open my umbrella, and make my way through the rain over the wet, muddy streets to my home.

"Good afternoon, Elsa," Sarah greets me as I step into the hallway.

"Hi Sarah, how was your day?" I ask automatically.

"Good," says Sarah. Then, whispering, "At least until the twins came home."

"What happened now?" I ask, agitated.

"The girls brought a mouse home, and it jumped on the floor in the living room. It's now under the cupboard, and the twins are trying to catch it, but so far without success. Your mother had a nervous fit and is upstairs in bed."

I don't listen to what else Sarah has to say and storm into the living room. The two girls are lying on their stomachs in front of the cupboard, poking with a broom handle underneath.

"Close the door," Jasmin yells, "or it'll escape!"

I close the door behind me, but almost immediately, it opens again. Dad is standing in the doorway. He has just come home from work too.

"Close the door, please!" Jasmin yells again.

Dad closes the door. "What's going on here?" he grumbles.

"They brought a mouse, and it's now under the cupboard," I explain.

"Girls," Dad says, "leave that animal alone. It will come out from under there when it gets hungry. By the way, how did you get that animal?"

Rose and Jasmin chatter at the same time.

Dad looks at me. "I see you've had another trying day," he says.

I nod, too tired to say anything.

"And you," Dad says to the twins, "will get a long list of chores to do this week."

The verdict is met with a lot of grumbling from the twins.

That night, I wake up with a start. Do I hear gnawing and squeaking? I lie still for a moment but hear nothing more. Who cares, I think indifferently and turn over onto my other side.

It's an exhausting year. I'm so overwhelmed that I almost want to look for another job.

"No, Elsa," Dad says, "after this school year, when the twins move to the next class, everything will return to normal. Hang in there a bit longer. I'll have a serious talk with the girls."

I nod resignedly. Rose's behaviour isn't the only thing that makes me feel gloomy. I miss Kate. I miss Paul.

Midway through the school year, Ms. Jones becomes ill. Her condition is serious enough that she can't return to school anytime soon. The headmaster takes over her class. For a few weeks, things go well, although it's evident to us as teachers that handling so much extra work is a heavy burden for him. He becomes irritable and impatient.

In the spring, during one of the lunch breaks in the staff room, the headmaster stands up and, in his authoritative tone, announces, "I think it's best if Ms. Jones's class gets a new teacher. Next Monday, Edward Elder will take over the class while Ms. Jones is unable to come to school."

Edward turns out to be a pleasant young man my age. With Ms. Jones no longer around to chat with during breaks, I naturally find myself spending more time with Edward. We sit next to each other in the staff room and are scheduled for playground duty at the same times. It's nice to have someone to talk to during the school days. It makes the days I'm dealing with the twins a bit easier and lighter.

"What are your plans for Dominion Day?" Edward asks me during one of the breaks. The first day of July is quickly approaching, marking the beginning of summer vacation.

"What's going on that day?" I ask.

"In the morning, there's a military parade with music, in the afternoon there's a concert at the bandstand at the corner of Granville and Georgia Street, and of course, there will be fireworks at the harbour when it gets dark," Edward replies.

"Maybe we should do everything," I say suddenly, feeling enthusiastic. "We could have a picnic in the park at lunchtime. Do you mind if I ask Kate and Dylan to join us?"

"Sure," says Edward. "That sounds like a great idea."

That Friday evening, when I visit Kate with the twins, I ask if she and Dylan would like to join Edward and me for the festivities. We agree to meet at my parents' house and go out together. The twins whine about whether they can come, too.

"You'll have to ask Mom and Dad," I fend them off.

The first thing the girls do when we get home is bombard Mom and Dad with the question of whether they can join Kate and me or not.

"No way," says Dad. "You can come with Mom and me, but you'll leave Elsa alone on the first day of vacation. She's had enough to deal with you two this past school year."

Deep in my heart, I am grateful for Dad's decision. The school year has exhausted me, and I look forward to a day out without the kids.

The sun shines cheerfully on the first day of July. The four of us walk to the street where the parade will pass. In the distance, we hear the bagpipes and see the soldiers approaching. The sun glints off the buttons on the soldiers' uniforms and the drums of the band that follows them. The wailing sound of the bagpipes cuts through my head as the musicians pass by. The military parade must be bringing back memories for Dylan. He stands with a sombre look as the parade marches by. We follow the parade to the harbour, where the soldiers and the band set up. After a speech by the mayor, we sing the Canadian national anthem.

O Canada!
Our home and native land!
True patriot love in all of us command.
With glowing hearts we see thee rise,
The True North strong and free!
From far and wide,
O Canada, we stand on guard for thee.
God keep our land glorious and free!
O Canada, we stand on guard for thee.

The crowd disperses once the ceremony is over.

"Shall we find a spot by the harbour for our picnic?" Kate suggests.

Under the shade of a tree, we spread out the quilt we brought and set down our baskets with treats. I pour lemonade into cups, and Kate hands out cookies sweetened with maple syrup. A little later, I let myself lie back. The warm sun, the sound of the rippling water, and the murmur of the festival-goers in the background make me drowsy. I enjoy the day off and the prospect of starting a new class in a few weeks and sending the twins over to a different teacher. For a moment, I feel a pang of missing someone, but I don't let that overshadow the enjoyment of the day.

Edward takes out his pocket watch. "It's about time to head to the concert."

We pack up the cups and plates and fold up the quilt. Dylan and Edward walk ahead, chatting happily as we make our way through the cheerful streets to the bandstand.

"Is Edward someone you might be interested in?" Kate asks. "He's a nice guy. He'd make a suitable marriage candidate."

"Maybe," I brush off. "He's definitely a nice guy, but I don't think he can replace Paul," I say.

"How long are you going to wait for Paul? He keeps traveling to some distant place, and you don't see him for weeks, sometimes months," Kate tries to convince me of a bleak future with Paul.

"Today, I want to enjoy my vacation," I say wearily. "Let's not talk about this difficult subject."

By now, we have arrived at the square where the concert will take place. Several people have brought their wooden chairs and are waiting on the street in front of the bandstand for the concert to start. We find a quiet spot from which we can hear and see everything well.

Afterward, we buy some food from a stand and wander toward the place where the fireworks will be set off. Dusk is setting in, and soon, dazzling illuminations fill the air. It's a spectacular display in the darkening sky.

After saying goodbye to Kate and Dylan, Edward takes me home. We walk arm in arm through the streets. My feet feel sore from all the walking today. Edward carries the picnic basket on his other arm.

"It was a really nice day," I sigh. "Thank you for your company today," I say as we stand in front of my parents' house.

"It was my pleasure," says Edward. "Maybe we can do something together again sometime?" he asks expectantly.

I nod somewhat hesitantly. "Sure," I eventually say. I feel confused and think of Paul. How long do I have to wait for him to stay home for good?

Edward tips his hat and heads home through the sparsely lit streets of the city.

"Did you have a nice day?" Mom asks as I enter the living room. She and Dad are reading by the floor lamp. "Edward's a nice young man," she adds with a telling expression.

I nod. "Yes, we had a very pleasant, enjoyable day. My feet are sore," I say, laughing as I kick off my shoes.

"Edward would be a suitable man for you, don't you think?" Mom says.

"Come on, Mom, Kate said that too. Don't ruin this nice day by talking about such a difficult subject."

Dad intervenes. "Elsa, don't worry. You're still young, you have a nice job, and you have us. What more do you need? A man will come later."

I look at him gratefully. "I think I'll go to bed," I announce. I wish my parents goodnight and head upstairs. It takes a while before I fall asleep. I keep tossing and turning. The thought of my future won't leave my mind. Is it wise to wait for Paul? Should I focus on Edward and see if I feel anything for him? No matter how much I worry, I can't figure it out.

I've taken up the habit of visiting Paul's grandmother every week. She misses her grandson. When I'm with her, it feels as though Paul is closer. We drink tea and chat about all sorts of things. Her eyesight is deteriorating, so I always read out loud the letters Paul sent her.

This week, I talk endlessly about the fun things I did on Dominion Day. When I mention that I spent the day with Edward, Kate, and Dylan, Grandma is silent for a moment.

I'm worried I have said too much. "Are you bothered that I spent the day with Edward?" I ask, concerned.

"No, dear, not at all. You can't wait indefinitely for my grandson. I would love to have you as a granddaughter, but if Paul doesn't take a step in the right direction, he'll lose his opportunity," Grandma says.

She places an envelope on the table. "Would you still read this letter to me?" she asks.

"Oh, of course," I reply. I open the envelope and take out Paul's letter. For a moment, my worries vanish as I read the cheerful letter, filled with his sometimes bizarre adventures. "He'll be coming home in a few weeks," I read with joy in my voice.

A smile also appears on Grandma's face.

During an enjoyable walk with Paul along the coast and the boats, I forget all the troubles of the past year. Unfortunately, summer vacation ends quickly, and Paul receives a new assignment. I ask him once more if he ever thinks about staying in Vancouver, but his answer is the same. "There's so much to experience in the world. I'm too young to settle down anywhere. Besides, they need me at the newspaper."

I don't say much. Does he even understand that I'm waiting for him and would like him to stay here? It seems like he doesn't realize it.

The new school year begins, and naturally, I find myself spending time with Edward again. He often walks part of the way with me after school. On a windy autumn day, as we are leaving the school, Paul is unexpectedly waiting there.

"Hey, Paul, it's great to see you," I say happily when I see him standing there. I introduce the two young men to each other, and the three of us walk home together. At a large intersection, our paths diverge, and Edward takes another route.

"See you tomorrow!" Edward waves.

I wave back.

"Hmm," says Paul, "that string bean seems interested in you."

"Indeed," I say as casually as possible.

"And," Paul probes, "do you go out with him?"

"Why do you want to know?" I ask somewhat defiantly.

Paul is silent for a moment. "You're right, it's none of my business," he finally says.

We continue walking in silence. At the intersection near my house, we say goodbye.

I'm unsure whether to visit Grandma that week, but I decide to go anyway. I tell her about my dilemma with Edward and Paul.

"It's a shame that young man is so restless," she says, referring to Paul. "I understand that you want to move on with your life, but marrying someone like Edward while your heart is with another is not wise," warns Grandma. "It's not fair to any of you."

In the following months, I notice that Paul writes less frequently. Responding to his letters becomes a burden. How can I fully commit to Paul when he doesn't commit to me? I love him; I would love nothing more than to pledge myself to him. Meanwhile, it is Edward with whom I spend time daily, talking and laughing. What path should I take?

 ❦

"Will you hold him for a moment?"
Without waiting for my answer, the young mother places her baby into my arms. The church service has just ended, and the congregation is slowly moving to the hall, where coffee is being served. The mother has her hands full with her toddler daughter, who is demanding attention. I look down at the baby boy's little face in my arms. Will I ever hold a child of my own? Before my thoughts can wander further, the mother takes her baby back. My arms feel empty, and for a moment, I stand there feeling lost.

Then my eye falls on Jasmin. She is now sixteen and growing into a beautiful young lady. She is talking with a boy who often seeks her attention during coffee at church. It wouldn't surprise me if something develops between them, I think to myself.

Near Jasmin, I see Edward with his wife. I feel a pang of pain deep inside, but then I pull myself together. During the year since we celebrated Dominion Day together, I realized that I had to make a choice. I decided to follow my heart, even though I knew it wouldn't be easy. With Edward, I would have a secure future; with Paul, everything was one big question mark. I could no longer bring myself to leave Edward hanging. I told him we could be friends but nothing more. Naturally, distance grew between us. At school, we no longer met every break. I missed the daily chats with Edward, but at the same time, I was relieved that a serious relationship was off the table.

My gaze drifts further and rests on Kate with her round belly. Last Friday evening, she proudly showed me the baby clothes she had sewn. She had to wait years for this pregnancy. I'm happy for her, but at the same time, I feel so alone. It seems as though everyone else's life is moving forward while mine stands still. The bright spots in my life are Paul's letters. Now that I have chosen to wait for him, I write to him every week, regardless of how often he writes himself. I must try to find peace with the fact that Paul cannot yet commit to me. When will the time be right? Will marriage ever fit into Paul's life?

Vancouver, 1900

I'm going for a few months to Europe... America... Ottawa..."

Each time I hear Paul say these words, I feel a lump in my throat. Fortunately, his letters always make me look forward to his return to Vancouver, helping to bridge the time of his absence. Sometimes I worry that our relationship will never progress beyond this ongoing correspondence we have already had for years. Occasionally, I dream about what it would be like to travel the earth with him, but I quickly push those thoughts aside. How could I leave my family behind to wander the world? Meanwhile, Paul travels to distant places, and I pray every evening for his safe return.

The twins, who no longer dance and jump so much but are trying to act like young ladies, visit Kate with me every Friday evening. On Sundays after church, Dylan, Kate, and their children, Daisy and Bobby, come to our home for coffee. Slowly, over time, Kate has become quieter. Caring for the little ones consumes her, but it's not just that. Over the years, Dylan has turned into a grumpy man, giving short answers to Dad's questions. His leg still bothers him significantly, and he's frustrated that he's stuck here while his friends, Paul and Fred, travel the world and have all sorts of experiences.

Years pass. I long for change but don't see how it could ever happen. The idea of resigning myself to a life of loneliness often confronts me head-on. Then, suddenly, with the turn of the century, change arrives. Life becomes a roller coaster that our family is carried away by, without any control over the ride. First, a letter from Paul arrives, saying that he will return to Vancouver and stay here for a while. Not long after, Fred reappears out of the blue after years, setting off a fiery chain of events.

❧

It's late October when Paul arrives in Vancouver. During my weekly visit to Grandma, Paul is also there.

"My grandmother is getting very old, but she's still quite lively," he confides in me as Grandma heads to the kitchen to pour coffee. "I've missed her cooking."

I nod. "I understand. Tell me about your experiences," I say with curiosity.

"I'll tell you what happened this week," Paul says. "The day after my arrival, I went to the Vancouver Weekly Herald office. I sat down with the editor and was assigned to cover news in the city. A lot has changed since I was away. As you know, the Vancouver of our childhood is gone. The city, with its trams and horse-drawn carriages, has become busy and hurried, just like all other large cities in the world.

Before I went hunting for news, I stopped by Dylan's prospector's shop to say hello. Dylan was talking to a man who looked vaguely familiar. I wandered around the shop, checking out new products.

"Hey Paul," I suddenly heard Dylan say behind me. "You remember Fred, don't you?"

I turned around and saw Fred's grin. I extended my hand, which he refused to shake.

"Well," I said, "back in town, eh?"

"I've had enough of the cold north. For now, I've made enough money."

"Good," I said, leaving it at that.

"Come have a beer," Fred said to Dylan.

72

Dylan hesitated. "I'm not sure that's a good idea," he said. "Kate and the kids are waiting at home for me so we can have dinner together."

"One beer shouldn't be a problem," Fred sneered. "Can't you spare a drink for your old buddy? Come on, man, don't be so childish."

Dylan gave in. "Okay, just one beer. Are you coming?" he asked me.

I hesitated, but I agreed. I was curious about Fred's stories and thought it wouldn't hurt to support Dylan morally. It was a good thing I went along. Dylan, no longer used to drinking, quickly became inebriated. The two drunks reminisced about bizarre memories. Unfortunately, it didn't stay at just one beer. It turned into so many that Dylan had to be helped home.

"It's getting late, Dylan. Let's go home," I insisted.

Together we trudged through the darkened streets of Vancouver, Dylan heavily leaning on my shoulder. We left Fred, who was intoxicated, behind in the pub.

Kate opened the door when I knocked.

"Oh no," she said, shocked. "What happened to him?"

"A bit too much beer," I said apologetically.

I helped Dylan inside and let him sink into an armchair.

"Just let him stay here tonight," I said to Kate. "Sorry."

With a gnawing feeling of guilt, I walked out of the living room to the front door. I closed it gently behind me and took a deep breath of the fresh sea breeze blowing over the city. I hope Dylan behaves better in the future and that Fred leaves town soon," Paul concludes his story.

"I hope so too," I say softly, shocked by the tale. I haven't spoken to Kate yet this week, and I'm unsure if she will mention this incident.

I'm glad Paul is back in town. It looks like he'll be staying here for a while now that he's covering the city news. He often picks me up from school, and we take walks along the beach to collect stones. I really enjoy these walks with him. Today is a rainy Friday. I close my classroom door and head home. The Chinese girl Lili, who lives not far from us, dances alongside me. She doesn't mind the rain, though her thin coat gets soaked. When we cross the street, she always takes my hand, afraid of the horse-drawn carriages and trams rushing through the city. At the T-junction, we each go our separate ways. Lili waves goodbye until the corner of the street where I live. I wave one last time before turning the corner.

Lili is the only child of Chinese parents who work hard for lower wages than Canadians. There is a lot of hostility toward Asian immigrants, and people in British Columbia fear that their jobs will be taken by them. Still, Lili's parents always smile whenever I see them.

Tonight, I'm visiting Kate again, and I hope Paul will come by too. He always shares fascinating stories about the people he interviews and the adventures he has on his travels.

After dinner, I help Mom clear the table. Sarah has the weekend off and has gone to visit her family.

"I'm going to Kate's," I say.

"We're coming too!" shout the twins from the top of the carved staircase.

Immediately, they run down, their wide skirts fluttering around their legs. We walk arm in arm to Kate's house.

"Do you hope Paul will be there?" Rose asks, eager for some romantic excitement.

"It's always nice when he is," I say as neutrally as possible.

"See," she whispers to Jasmin, "she still likes him."

I suppress a smile and let the two girls gossip.

Kate has just finished cleaning up the dishes. Daisy helps her place the last plates in the cupboard.

"Come on," Daisy says to the twins, "I want to show you what I made at school this week."

The twins follow Daisy into the living room. I'm alone with Kate in the kitchen.

"How's it going?" I ask, noticing Kate's pale face.

"Good," she says apathetically.

"And how's Dylan? Is he avoiding that dull Fred a bit?"

Kate shakes her head. "No, that guy comes here far too often."

Immediately, there's a knock at the door, and I hear voices outside.

"I'll open it," I say and hurry to the front door.

Without waiting for me to let him in, Fred steps past me into the hallway. In the living room, I hear him greet Dylan loudly.

"Hi," I say to Paul, who has arrived with Fred.

I take his wet coat and hang it on a hook in the hallway.

"Catch," Fred calls from the living room door, throwing his coat at me.

I just manage to catch it. For a moment, I stand bewildered with the dirty, wet coat in my hands, then I throw it into a corner under the coat rack. Paul looks at me with raised eyebrows and bursts into laughter. We walk into the living room together.

Dylan stirs the fire a bit, and I help Kate serve the coffee and homemade butter cake. Paul compliments Kate on the delicious cake. Fred and Dylan are engaged in an animated conversation, digging into the cake without a word of thanks.

"Listen up," Fred says, looking around the group. "I've got some news."

"What is it?" the twins ask in unison.

"On a mountain on Vancouver Island," Fred begins, "a grand discovery has been made."

"Have they found Bigfoot?" Rose asks excitedly.

"Oh, girl," Fred says disdainfully, "that's old news. That hairy fellow has been living there for centuries. No, it's something much more important."

He pauses to see if he has everyone's attention and continues: "There was a huge fire on that mountain last summer. Not unusual, but when those men who had to run for their lives returned weeks later, they found a large piece of copper exposed by the fire. Now, they've started dividing the mountain into sections, and we can begin mining for copper and gold there. Are you coming with me, Dylan?" Fred says, nudging Dylan's shoulder. "It'll make us a fortune."

I see Kate looking alarmed. "Dylan, no!" she says, but he doesn't listen. Dylan's curiosity is piqued, and he asks Fred all sorts of details.

"Paul," I whisper, "can you convince Dylan to stay here?"

"Mind your own business," says Dylan, who overheard me. "I can decide for myself whether I'm going or not."

I keep quiet, but now Kate also tries to persuade him to reconsider. "You have a good job here," she begins, "why would you give it up for something you're not sure will bring you anything?"

Dylan ignores her and adds more wood to the fire. "I'll think about it," he says to Fred as he heads home.

I cling to Paul once more as he, also, prepares to leave. "Can't you do something to stop him?"

He shrugs. "He probably won't listen to me. It's even possible that I'll have to go, too. I've heard about the gold rush. The paper wants to send someone, and I'm the journalist with the most experience in gold mining."

I sigh. "Come on, girls," I say to the twins, "we're heading home."

I look sadly at Kate. "I hope it all turns out alright and that Dylan isn't foolish enough to give up his job," I say to her.

"I hope so, too," she says wearily. She stands up and whispers to me, "Since Fred has come back in the picture, Dylan has been so closed off to me. He won't listen to any ideas I suggest and is sometimes just downright rude. That Fred has a bad influence on him."

We hug, and I head home with the twins. Paul walks with us for a while, each arm linked with one of the twins.

"Paul," says Rose, ever straightforward, "which one of us would you choose as a girlfriend, Jasmin or me?"

"Girl, what kind of question is that?" I say.

Paul laughs heartily. "I think I'd choose someone a bit older than you."

"Someone like Elsa?" Rose counters.

Paul looks at me with a smile. I feel a blush creeping onto my cheeks and am glad we've just passed a streetlight, with the next one a bit farther away.

"It has to be someone who wants to travel the world. I'm not sure Elsa would want to give up her teaching job for that."

I stay silent, but thoughts race through my head. Would I really want to give up my job for him? Would I want to be constantly moving from one place to another? Could I leave my family for months at a time? I'm not at all sure I can. On the other hand… I haven't been enjoying my work as much as I used to lately. The headmaster and a few of my male colleagues aren't exactly friends. Sometimes I'm fed up with the subtle, humiliating criticism directed at women. Is that a good reason to travel the world, following a man who never knows where he'll be the next month? Or should I stay here waiting for a man whose return is always uncertain? I can't figure it out.

We say goodbye on the corner, where we each go our separate ways. Paul goes to his grandmother's, and we head home to Mom and Dad.

The following week, Kate bursts into our house in tears. "Dylan had taken a day off work and went with Fred to Victoria to buy a piece of land on Mount Sicker," she shares. "He casually told me that he's leaving this weekend and expects me to follow soon because he can't afford to maintain two houses," Kate sobs. "He's spent most of my inheritance to make the purchase," she adds desperately.

Even Dad, who is usually good at coming up with solutions, has nothing to say and stares into the fire.

I feel terribly for Kate. Then, on an impulse, I respond, "I'll help you move. Christmas vacation is almost here, and we can go then." I try to sound as determined as possible. Kate needs support, and I can offer that.

"Oh dear," Mom cries, "can't you move in with us with the children?"

"No, Mom," Kate says, "I don't want to be a burden on you. It's not good for your nerves to have three extra people in the house."

I put an arm around Kate. "It will be alright," I whisper. Deep down, I'm not so sure.

At the schoolyard gate, I'm greeted by Lili. The girl is always the first to arrive at school.

"May I help you set out the books and notebooks?" She dances around me.

"Of course," I say with a smile.

Together, we climb the few steps leading to the school's front door. In the large, high hallway, Lili hangs her coat on one of the small hooks meant for the children. I walk to the end of the hall. My heels click on the grey-white tiled floor of the still-quiet school. I open the door to the staff room and peek around the corner.

"Good morning," I say to the headmaster, who is hunched over a stack of papers on his desk.

He looks up at me with a frown over the glasses perched on the tip of his nose. "You're early," he greets me back.

"I wanted to speak with you for a moment," I say. "I wanted to let you know that I will be going to Vancouver Island over the Christmas vacation to help my sister and the children move. They are moving to the mining town on Mount Sicker."

The frown on the headmaster's forehead deepens. He knows Kate and Dylan well, and Daisy and Bobby go to school here. He looks at me searchingly. "Something tells me you plan to stay there longer than just for the vacation."

"No, no," I hasten to say. "I just don't know how long they will need my help. Life in a mining town doesn't seem so easy, especially in the winter."

"We all know that life in mining towns is tough. Why are you going if the conditions are so miserable there?"

"I want to help my sister during that first period," I reply.

"You know," says the headmaster as he adjusts his glasses, "it's their own choice to go in search of wealth. It's not your responsibility to solve their problems."

"I know that," I defend myself, "but she is my sister after all. Besides, it wasn't her choice to go there. She's married, and

79

her husband and his friend decided to leave. What else can she do but go along?"

"If women want to be so compliant, they must also face the consequences," the headmaster says rudely.

"What!" I exclaim. "Is staying here and taking care of her children on her own such a good solution?"

"It's just a matter of what you want," the headmaster says wearily. "I need to get back to my paperwork." With that, he cuts off the conversation.

My eyes flash with anger. "As if women have the right to make such choices in this society," I mumble indignantly as I turn around.

I see the teacher of the second-highest class walk into the hallway. I let him into the staff room. I pause at the door for a moment. An animated conversation develops between the headmaster and the teacher.

"Paperwork, huh?" I mutter.

Disappointed and disdainful, I cast one more look at the two and then turn to Lili, who is looking up at me expectantly.

"Come on," I say to the child, "you can get the notebooks ready. I'll make a drawing on the board."

Lili skips ahead of me, and together we prepare the classroom for the upcoming lessons. Throughout the day, I keep glancing at the clock. The children are restless. They, like me, are counting the days until the Christmas vacation. After lunch, the wealthiest boy in the class raises his hand. "Miss, we're going to Whistler to ski." He looks around the class, challengingly.

"Oh, how nice," I say. Then I ask, "Are there any more children who want to share what they will be doing during the Christmas vacation?"

A few hands go up. A boy hopes for a thick layer of snow this year. His cousin is coming to visit, and he wants to build a snow fort with him. A girl is looking forward to the Christmas celebration at the church. She loves singing Christmas carols. She loves the smell of home-baked cookies.

"Miss," the quiet boy in the class then asks, looking at me intently, "what will you be doing during the vacation?"

Then I tell them about the mining town where they've found gold, silver, and copper, and where Daisy and Bobby will be moving.

The students know my niece and nephew. They listen attentively, and then the Wild West stories come out about relatives who also caught gold fever and went to the Klondike. I have to laugh a little now and then.

"Hmm," I say as a boy stands up and tells a story about miners fighting each other for the bit of gold found by someone else. "It can't be that bad, can it?"

The boy responds indignantly, "My uncle has been there himself. He saw it with his own eyes."

I soothe him. "Sit down," I gesture. "Luckily, I haven't heard such stories about Mount Sicker yet."

"Oh," the boy assures me, "that will come."

A cold shiver runs down my spine, and I pull my sleeves a bit farther over my wrists. Then I clap my hands. It's time for music class.

"Yes!" says the girl who loves singing happily.

Together, we practice the Christmas carols that we'll sing next Friday, the last school day of the year.

After school, Paul is waiting for me. I'm pleasantly surprised. Together we walk home.

"As I expected," says Paul, "the newspaper wants me to go to Mount Sicker to write about the mining town. So, we can travel together," he says, laughing.

"That will be a great relief for Mom and Dad, knowing that you're coming with us," I say. I'm relieved too. After all, Kate and I will have to see what we find at Mount Sicker, and Paul will be more of a support to us than Fred and Dylan.

ഔ

That Friday before Christmas, there is an excited atmosphere at school. The children are fidgeting in their seats with impatience for the upcoming Christmas party. In the morning, I leave the math books put away in the cabinet. I tell the Christmas story of the baby Jesus in the manger and the shepherds who believed the message of the angels and came to the stable to worship the baby. The students listen breathlessly. Several children are sucking their thumbs, dreaming away on the images evoked by the sound of my voice.

After the story, I hand out drawing sheets. "Draw what you remember from the Christmas story," I say.

Immediately, the first students bend over their sheets of paper, and I hear pencils scratching. It doesn't take long before tongues are sticking out of various children's mouths, and some students are scratching frantically at their hair. I enjoy the enthusiasm with which the children have started. Mary, Joseph, and the baby Jesus appear on the sheets in a wooden stable, surrounded by cows and donkeys. In the background, mountains appear with snow-capped peaks. Shepherds with sheep and skies full of angelic hosts make the drawings shine. The quiet boy of the class draws shepherds peeking through their fingers at the angels.

"They must have been very impressed," he whispers as I walk by.

I place my hand briefly on his small shoulder. "I think you're right," I say.

I walk around the tables, praising the children. Meanwhile, my eyes keep going to the clock. Just a few more hours, and then it's vacation.

After lunch, all the schoolchildren put on their warm coats. In the schoolyard, they form a long line, two by two. When the headmaster has locked the door, the entire line serpentine-like walks behind him to the church, which is a few streets away. I walk in the middle of the line with a child on each hand. In the church, the children take the front pews. Parents and grandparents fill the rest of the church. My parents, and Rose and Jasmin have also come. The headmaster tells the Christmas story. The children sing the songs they've practiced. I look around the church and nod to a few parents. I gently nudge the shoulder of the boy in front of me in the pew, who is fidgeting. The quiet boy of the class studies the ceiling as if angelic hosts are floating there. Afterward, there is a variety of yummy treats in the large hall of the church. Mothers have brought trays of cinnamon cookies and pots of hot chocolate.

I am offered a cookie by Lili.

"Thank you for everything you've taught me this past year," she says, making a polite bow.

"Thank you for being such a good student and for helping me so often in the mornings," I reply with a smile and bow as well.

The young teacher from the second grade stands next to me at the cookie and hot chocolate table. "That was a good ending to the past year," he says to me as we enjoy a cup of cocoa.

I nod. "It certainly was."

I leave it at that. I don't find it necessary to encourage him in his attempt to capture my attention.

❧

It's Friday evening now. Mom has sent Sarah home for the Christmas holidays. The twins are baking cookies, and I'm making the pudding. The turkey we had plucked goes into a well-sealed zinc tub in the shed until tomorrow. The shed is securely locked to keep out bears, cougars, and wolves.

Aunt Margaret, Dad's sister, has taken the ferry from Vancouver Island to spend Christmas with us. She's in the living room reminiscing about past Christmases with Mom and Dad. It's cozy, but I've retreated a bit.

"Is something wrong, Elsa?" Aunt Margaret asks. "You're so quiet."

"She's going to Vancouver Island after Christmas," says Dad.

"Vancouver Island?" Aunt Margaret asks, surprised. "What are you going to do there? And are you traveling with me? How nice!" she says enthusiastically.

"I'm going to help Kate and the children move to the mining town on Mount Sicker," I answer.

"Mount Sicker?" Aunt Margaret says, absorbed in thought. "You're going to Mount Sicker? Who was it that also went to Mount Sicker?" She frowns and puts her right index finger against the bridge of her nose. After thinking deeply, she suddenly perks up. "I remember now," she says. "My neighbour went there too. He's a teacher at the school there."

I look at her in surprise. "Maybe I'll meet him there. The town isn't very big, and Daisy and Bobby will surely go to the same school. Should I pass on your regards?" I suggest.

"Yes, yes, do that. Send him my warm regards," says Aunt Margaret.

84

She fills the next five minutes with extolling her neighbour, who is such a good guy.

When I later find myself in the kitchen with Mom working on dinner, I say, "I think I already find this 'good guy' to be rather unpleasant. He sounds too perfect."

Mom smiles and surprises me by saying, "Don't judge just yet. He's probably not a pushover; otherwise, he wouldn't have taken a job in such a dirty, grimy mining town."

Kate, the children, Paul, and his grandmother are also coming for Christmas. The house fills with laughter and giggles as Daisy and Bobby play games devised by Rose and Jasmin.

"I've heard," says Dad to Paul, "that you're going to the mining town too."

"Indeed," says Paul, "I thought it would be wise to travel directly with Kate, Elsa, and the children."

"I'm glad you'll be keeping an eye on things. I don't like the idea of women going to such a town," says Dad.

"You're probably right," says Paul, "if it's anything like Klondike, they won't have an easy time. Don't worry," he adds quickly when he sees a deep wrinkle forming above Dad's nose. "I'll stay close to them."

"Thank you," says Dad while he briefly places his hand on Paul's shoulder.

After Christmas, we say goodbye to Mom, Dad, and the twins and take the tram to the ferry.

"I've had a few wonderful days at your home," says Aunt Margaret.

"I was very glad you visited," I say to her.

When we arrive at the ferry, all the freight and mail for Vancouver Island has already been loaded onto the ship. A crew member comes to warn us that the boat will be leaving soon.

The children run up the gangway, followed by Aunt Margaret, Kate, Paul, and me at a slower pace. We seize a spot along the railing next to other passengers waving to their family members. The steam whistle blasts into the air, and slowly the ferry pulls away from the wooden dock.

We hurry inside, to the warmth and the delicious smell of coffee and pastries.

Aunt Margaret has taken the liberty of ordering for us, and just as we sit down, a waitress brings the requested coffee and cookies.

I cradle my warm coffee cup with both hands and take a small sip.

"Are you all ready for lunch?" Aunt Margaret asks a little later.

"But, Aunt Margaret," I say, "I've just finished my coffee and cookies."

"I," says Paul with his cheerful smile, "I'd like something.'

Aunt Margaret beckons the waitress and orders lunch without regard for my full stomach.

"It will be hours before we reach our destination," she defends her decision to order a meal. "You can't travel on an empty stomach."

Aunt Margaret turns to Paul. "Your newspaper assignment came at just the right time for Kate and Elsa's parents. Now they can let their daughters and grandchildren go to that mining town with peace of mind. Surely you won't betray that trust, young man?" she adds in a serious tone.

"No, no, ma'am," Paul hastens to assure her. "They'll be in good hands with me." A grin appears on his face.

Aunt Margaret looks at him sternly, and his face becomes more serious. He must feel uncomfortable under her intense gaze.

"Very well," she says slowly, stirring the soup the waitress has just placed in front of her.

After that, we sit in silence for a while, enjoying the vegetable soup and salmon salad.

The engine in the belly of the boat churns and propels the vessel through the ocean. Thick grey clouds hang over the waves. The guests at the other tables chat and laugh.

"Do you see that distinguished gentleman at the table with those flamboyant ladies?" Aunt Margaret asks Kate and me, leaning toward us.

I look in the direction where loud laughter comes from. Paul turns around as well.

At the table in question sits an affluent gentleman surrounded by four extravagantly dressed ladies.

"You call that distinguished?" I ask Aunt Margaret. "A man who associates with such women?"

"Doesn't he look distinguished?" she replies. "He's the head of a large mining company on the island. And those ladies, he uses them to keep his workers in line. He himself will not use their services. He's not that foolish. He knows very well that he could catch a terrible disease from them."

"But," I ask, in my ignorance, "can't his workers get very sick too?"

"They do," she confirms, "but workers are easier to replace than a boss."

"But," I insist, "those ladies can get sick too."

"Yes," Paul now joins the conversation, "those girls don't live long."

I fall silent and stare at the noisy group. Inside, I feel disgust at the behaviour of that man and irritation at those women. How can they be so foolish as to waste their lives?

It seems Paul reads my thoughts. "They have little choice," he says in a tone that seems to reflect concern as well. "They can do laundry for the rich for $12 a week and always have cracked hands and a sore back, or entertain ten customers each evening for $12 per person," he says glumly.

"Tastes differ," I say bitterly.

"Will you come with us to the mining town first before continuing on to Victoria?" Paul asks Aunt Margaret.

"Oh, certainly not!" exclaims Aunt Margaret. "I'm going straight to my own hovel."

I laugh. Aunt Margaret's 'hovel' is almost a castle, where she lives with many servants. Next year, it will be our turn to spend Christmas with her. It's just that Mom and Dad don't want to go there every year, but if it were up to me, I would spend every Christmas there.

Three hours later, the ferry docks at the port of Ladysmith. Everyone grabs their suitcases and disembarks. Paul helps Kate carry her heavy trunk. We walk to the train station and see a timetable on the wall showing the train's arrival and departure times.

The train will depart for Victoria at four o'clock. Kate, the children, Paul, and I only need to travel for an hour. Aunt Margaret still has three hours before she arrives in Victoria. Fortunately, we don't have to wait long. It's already late in the afternoon, so we sit on the wooden benches in the warm waiting area until the train from the north, coming from Nanaimo, arrives. The small space is crowded. The distinguished gentleman and the ladies attract a lot of attention, but they don't seem to care.

Children are whining, tired from the long ferry ride. Most passengers are people returning from visiting friends and family on the mainland, as evident from their dressy clothing.

The group of young men joking with each other are probably here for work. Maybe they work in forestry or mining and are returning from a well-deserved vacation after weeks of hard physical labor.

We hear the distant whistle of the approaching train. We pick up our suitcases and join the other passengers outside. Thick clouds of smoke billow from the chimney of the black locomotive. The huge grill glides over the tracks in front of the wheels. The bright light at the front of the train beams through the oncoming twilight. Once again, the steam whistle shrieks: "Get out of the way, make way." Hissing, the locomotive comes to a stop by the platform. I see soot-streaked faces above in the locomotive. A door opens, and a nimble young man jumps out.

"We have a few minutes before the train departs again," says the conductor as he walks down the line of waiting people.

"Come on," says Paul, tugging at my sleeve. "Let's find a spot on the train."

He helps Kate and Aunt Margaret with their suitcases and baggage.

"Stay close," Kate warns the children.

I follow the group, half stumbling in the crowd of people getting on and off. I clutch the handle of my suitcase, afraid it might catch on something and I'll drop it.

Paul jumps onto the train and offers Aunt Margaret his hand. She grabs it and pulls herself up the steps. The children jump onto the train by themselves. Kate and I also receive a hand from Paul.

In the middle of the carriage, two benches facing each other are free. Paul lifts the suitcases onto the rack above our heads, and we sit down on wooden benches once again. Kate's trunk is too large and remains in the space near the doors.

My rear feels like a plank, and I sit stiffly upright against the high backrest that extends well above my head. I sit by one of the windows. Aunt Margaret sits across from me, with Kate next to her holding Daisy on her lap. Paul sits next to me and pulls Bobby onto his lap.

I draw my winter coat tightly around me. A cold wind blows past my ankles through the outside door that is still open.

The conductor's whistle pierces through the darkening winter afternoon. "All aboard," he calls out loudly, and then he jumps onto the train himself.

The locomotive starts chugging. The waiting room glides past us. People wave.

Through one of the windows, I catch a glimpse of the ocean, with grey clouds hanging above. A single light from a boat twinkles above the water. It quickly becomes too dark to see anything outside, and all that remains is the illuminated carriage bumping through the evening. The children doze off to the rocking of the train. I feel sleepy too and stare at the reflection of the people on the train. Slowly, my eyes close. I still hear Aunt Margaret and Paul starting a conversation in the distance, though I have no idea what it's about.

I wake with a start as the train begins to brake sharply and the whistle blares.

"Well," says Aunt Margaret, "this is where you all get off. I'll keep going for a few more hours."

We wait for the train to stop. Paul retrieves our suitcases from the racks above the seats. He politely shakes Aunt Margaret's hand and bows slightly. "It was pleasant spending the Christmas holidays and making this trip with you," he says. "Hopefully, we'll see you again."

"Take good care of my nieces and nephew," she insists.

"I will," he promises.

We give Aunt Margaret a big hug and walk down the path to the outside door.

I jump off the train, and my feet sink into the muddy ground. I see nothing but dark bushes and trees.

The train moves again, and I wave to Aunt Margaret. She doesn't wave back. She probably can't see us standing in the pitch black.

The distinguished gentleman, the ladies, and the group of young men have also disembarked.

In the light of the departing train, we see a road running perpendicular to the tracks. Several carts are waiting to transport passengers.

"Come on," Paul commands, "let's try to get a spot on one of the carts."

Apparently, they had anticipated the number of people coming by train, and there is plenty of room on the carts. The distinguished gentleman and his ladies take the front cart, and we join two young men in the next cart. The rest of the group of young men gets into the third cart.

We've hardly started when Paul strikes up a conversation with the young men. "Where are you heading?" he asks.

"We're going to Mount Sicker. We spent the Christmas holidays with family. We're brothers," they explain. "Last summer, we bought a piece of land on Mount Sicker. We're digging there now."

"And," Paul asks curiously, "have you found anything yet?"

The brothers look at each other and grin. "We're not telling," they chuckle.

"I understand," says Paul. "I've been to Klondike. I didn't tell anyone what I found, either."

A lively conversation starts about the minerals being mined at Mount Sicker. They tell Paul about the gold and silver discoveries, and especially about the copper, which is transported in buckets by heavy cables through the air down to the train.

The horses pulling the cart make a left turn, and I bump into Paul. I quickly grab onto the bench for support. In the distance, I see the vague outline of a mountain with two humps against the dark sky.

"Look," says one of the young men, "that's Mount Prevost. Behind it is Mount Sicker."

I shiver and pull my coat tighter around me. Kate does the same. The children, sitting between us, are shivering.

"The end of the journey is in sight," I say to them.

I can't see much of the surroundings. It's pitch dark, and only the lamps at the front of the carts cast their light on the path. Here and there, I see a light flickering behind a farmhouse window or from a fire at the First Nations people who live here.

I feel the cart starting to tilt. We're going up the mountain. It takes almost an hour before we reach the mining village. During this time, I cling to the cart's rails to avoid constantly sliding into Paul. My hand and arm cramp up. Paul's arm is pressed tightly against my back, where he is also holding onto a rail so I have little room to move.

By early evening, we finally reach the top of the mountain. The carts stop in front of the village inn. Despite the cold, the horses are sweaty. The drivers throw warm blankets over their shiny backs, and in the light of the gas lamps in front of the pub, the passengers disembark from the carts. The cart with the distinguished gentleman and the ladies of the night continues on to the large hotel a bit farther down the road.

"Do you know Dylan?" Paul asks the two young men riding with us. "Do you know where he lives?"

"No idea," they say. "Maybe they know more at the pub."

"We'll ask inside," Paul says to us and resolutely steps into the pub.

We follow him hesitantly. The pub is crowded and warm. All the tables are occupied, and men with soot-streaked faces are hanging around the bar. There's laughter and conversation and playing cards being thrown on the tables. Most men have a large glass of beer in front of them. Apparently, the prohibition laws are not being observed here. All the police officers must be living down in Duncan. Kate, the children, and I stand behind Paul on the doormat and look around the pub. Several men look up from their card games.

Suddenly, I spot Dylan. He is sitting at a table for four at the far end of the room. I see Fred sitting with him. My brother-in-law doesn't notice us because he is facing away from the door. I recognize him by his spiky hair and slumped shoulders.

I nudge Kate. "Look, there's Dylan."

Kate and I immediately walk to Dylan's table. Paul stays by the door with the suitcases and the children, who are looking into the pub with wide, astonished eyes.

I tap Dylan on the back, and he turns around so quickly that I'm afraid he might hit me. Fred also looks up, grinning. I understand the reason for Dylan's startled reaction. The table is covered with coins, and there's a glass of alcohol in front of him.

"Hey," says Dylan. "I didn't expect you yet. Did you take the first ferry and train?" he asks nervously.

"That's right," I say, "and you must know how we can get to your tent."

"Yes, yes, of course," he says anxiously. "Let me just finish this game."

I'd prefer to drag him out of his chair and take him home rather than risk losing a day's wages at this gambling table in this smoky place. I restrain myself and walk back to Paul. Kate hesitates and stays with Dylan. I see her trying to convince him to stop playing, but he shakes his head in annoyance. Eventually, she gives up and comes over to us.

"He needs to finish his game," I say, scornfully. "If he's unlucky, all his wages will go up in smoke."

Kate has tears in her eyes. Paul says nothing. He takes in every detail of the pub. Suddenly, Dylan makes a brusque gesture, pushing his chair back, tossing his remaining cards on the table, yanking his coat from the back of the chair so that it almost tips over, and heads toward us. Without a word, he slams his shoulder against the door and goes outside. Outside, he puts on his coat.

"This way," he says, pointing with the cigarette butt he's holding between his fingers.

With the cigarette butt, he lights a lantern that's sitting on the ground against the wall of the pub. He grabs a handle of the trunk that Kate brought and gestures for her to take the other side. They walk into the darkness ahead of us.

Paul walks behind. "Shall I carry your suitcase for you?" he asks.

"No, it's fine, thank you," I say. Suddenly, I feel grateful for the kind gesture.

We trudge along behind Dylan and Kate, dragging our suitcases. The children are struggling to move through the thick layer of snow. My shoes are not made for walking in a mining village. It's hard to see where we're going in the dark. It rained heavily in Vancouver last week, but here on the mountain, which is situated much higher than Vancouver and the valley it stands along, snow has been lying for weeks. When we were driving up the mountain, I saw that the snow had formed a thin layer between the trees halfway up, but here it's at least a foot deep.

My shoes sink into the snow, and my feet become wet and cold. I slog through the snow dragging my suitcase and myself along. We have now left the main path and come upon a side path behind the hotel. Here and there, I see small lights between the seams of the tent doors. The men working on Mount Sicker usually live in tents. I hear Dylan telling Kate that he already has wood ready to build a cabin.

Paul is walking right behind me. He comes up beside me and grabs one of the handles of my suitcase. It's a bit awkward carrying the suitcase together, but it's very kind of him.

Dylan's cigarette is apparently done. He throws the butt away, making a small light in the disturbed snow.

It seems like the walk will never end. My feet are frozen. A strong wind tugs at my hat and skirts and bites at my face.

Then Dylan stops in front of a dirty white, fairly large, rectangular tent. A lamp hangs above the entrance. A piece of canvas flutters loose in the wind.

We leave the suitcases outside and go into the tent.

On the earthen floor in the middle of the tent, is a brazier with a small fire smoldering in it. Dylan adds new pieces of wood to the fire, making it blaze brighter.

In one corner of the tent, I see a pile of rags and blankets— probably Dylan's sleeping area.

"Come on," says Kate. "Let's put the suitcases inside and get our sleeping arrangements ready. Do you have anything we can eat?" she asks Dylan.

I bring the suitcases inside and start laying out the bedding. The children and Paul help me while Kate stirs the pot hanging from an iron tripod over the fire.

It doesn't smell bad. Kate busily prepares bowls and fills them with stew from the pot. We sit in a circle around the fire. The bowl Kate hands me feels very hot to my numb hands, so I set it down on the ground in front of me. The conversation isn't flowing. Paul asks Dylan various questions, but the answers he gets are curt. Around eight o'clock, Kate suggests we go to sleep. Everyone agrees. We've had a long journey, and Dylan has to get up early the next morning to go to work.

"Dylan," Paul asks, "can I stay here tonight and set up my tent next to yours tomorrow?"

Dylan nods. "Fine by me," he says.

It's an unusual concept to sleep in a tent with so many other people, which also doubles as our living and dining room.

Around the tent walls, the beds are now set up on the floor, all with their feet toward the fire. Above the fire is a hole in the tent roof where the smoke escapes through a pipe. Paul has placed my suitcase at the head of my bed. Outside, I hear an owl hooting, and distant sounds from the pub drift in. The fire crackles softly, and occasionally, a twig snaps with a pop, sending sparks flying.

Unfortunately, sleep won't come, no matter how tired I am. By the firelight, I see that Paul is also lying awake with his eyes open.

"Can't you sleep either?" I whisper.

Paul turns his head toward me and then lies on his side. Whispering, he says, "I found it heartbreaking to see Dylan's reaction to his wife and children arriving at the pub. They are clearly a burden to him—like a block on his leg. He would rather gamble and drink than care for his family. Apparently, he's stuck in Fred's grip."

"I'm troubled by it too," I whisper back. "I have no idea what I can do about it."

"Nothing, at the moment," says Paul. "Tomorrow, in daylight, we'll have a better picture of everything. Try to get some sleep, okay?"

"Okay," I whisper. "Good night."

It takes a while longer before I finally fall asleep.

When I wake up, I see that Paul's bed is empty.

At that moment, the tent flap opens, and Paul comes back inside. "I set up my tent next to the big one. There's already enough daylight to see what I'm doing," he says in a whisper so as not to wake everyone. "I made a fire in front of my tent like I used to in Klondike before I built a cabin. The difference is that it's already mid-winter now. I better come back here—the wind was blowing the smoke into my face and stinging my eyes no matter where I sat."

He settles back onto his bed. "I plan to write a few good articles as quickly as possible and then take you back to Vancouver. If I can, I'll also try to convince Kate and the kids to do the same."

"That's a good idea. I don't like the thought of staying here for long," I agree with him.

"After breakfast," Paul says softly, "when the mine whistle sounds, I'll head to the village. I want to talk to the men who work in the mines for the mining company, as well as those who are digging for themselves. Dylan and Fred belong to a third category — they're digging for themselves but not finding enough on their land, so they also work in the mines." Paul sighs. "I hope they'll tell me something more than the usual story about how everything in the mines is dirty and they're underpaid. Maybe I'll find people who can tell me something new, like the mine director. He probably won't be very talkative, but you never know." Shrugging, he adds, "I'll also try to talk to someone from the group of Chinese workers if I can find someone who speaks understandable English and is willing to trust me. It's not easy to infiltrate as an outsider. Maybe they can tell me something about the explosives they're using nowadays. That's their responsibility, after all."

Then he slips out of the tent again. "Just checking the fire," he whispers.

I smile at his enthusiasm.

As soon as Kate gets up and heads to the outhouse, I sit up and pull a comb from my travel bag. Sitting on my makeshift bed, I take out the braid I put in last night. I comb my hair and drape it loosely on both sides of my ears, pinning it up with a few combs at the back of my head. No one bothered to change into sleepwear the night before. I can't bear the thought of changing clothes with two grown men around. It wouldn't have been practical either, as even with the fire burning all night, it was cold and drafty in the tent.

I stand up and go to check on Kate. As soon as I close the tent flap behind me, I regret not putting on my coat. It's icy cold this early in the morning, and the biting wind blows fine snowflakes into my face.

The mountain looks very different in the morning light compared to the previous evening darkness. The sky is grey, and more snow is probably on the way. In the distance, in the valley below, I see the city of Duncan, where a few lights are burning here and there. I can't see much farther; the clouds are hanging low.

Then, the door of the small wooden building used as a toilet opens behind me.

Kate comes out.

I walk up to her. "Good morning," I greet her, giving her a big hug.

Kate smiles faintly.

I'm worried about her but say nothing. "I'm going to use the outhouse; I'll come help you with breakfast in a moment." I slip behind the door of the small building, and immediately, the awful smell from the hole in the ground hits me in the face. I hold my breath and hardly dare to look into the hole. Nevertheless, I do. About three meters below me, I see a pile of filth. Pieces of old newspapers are scattered in the pit on top of the excrement and urine of those who used it before me.

I grab my skirts and hoist them high. Then, I lean over the hole and force myself to relieve myself. Deep below, I hear it land with a soft patter on the pile. I fix my gaze on the heart-shaped hole in the door and stare at the stars still faintly visible in the sky. Balancing with my skirts in one hand and a piece of newspaper in the other, I quickly finish the toilet ritual.

I'm relieved to be back outside, with the cold, fresh wind blowing around my ears. I hurry back to the tent. As soon as I'm inside, Dylan gets up to go to the toilet as well. Good luck, I think derisively as I watch him disappear outside.

Kate is busy frying eggs and bacon in a pan.

Daisy is awake but still cozy in her warm bed.

"Hi, Aunt Elsa," she greets me.

"Good morning," I say. "Did you sleep well?"

"Pretty good," she replies.

"Kate, what can I do for you?" I ask.

"Not much right now. After breakfast, you can beat the blankets outside and sweep up. Daisy can help you with that. Then we'll head to the school in the mining village to see if I can enroll the children in classes," she says.

When Dylan and Paul return to the tent, we eat the scrambled eggs, which the hens behind the tent in a small coop have laid. Kate serves bacon and coarsely sliced bread alongside it.

"You should slaughter a few chickens," Dylan says to Kate. "They don't lay well in the winter, and we could use some extra meat."

After breakfast, Daisy and I take the blankets we slept on outside and shake them out vigorously. It's a good thing the tent door is closed because dust flies everywhere. We carry the blankets back inside and sweep the earthen floor of the tent before laying them down.

Meanwhile, Dylan has left for the mine, and Paul has headed to the village to look for news for his articles.

"Dylan has been so grumpy since he's been in contact with Fred again. He feels like everything is going wrong," Kate sighs softly so Daisy doesn't hear. "I don't know what to do. He drinks way too much. Fred has such a bad influence on him. I think it's forbidden to serve alcohol in the pub, but the officers must all live down in the town."

"I noticed that," I say, "when I saw the whole crowd in the pub last night. How many women are there in the mining village?"

"We're probably in the minority. From the ladies we saw with the mine director yesterday, we can't expect much support. They probably find it easy if the men drink a lot. Then they don't have to work too hard for their money," she says bitterly.

"It must be very dangerous for them, especially when the men are drunk," I say, worried. "Paul mentioned that the rooms are only separated by curtains, so the other girls can keep an eye on things if something goes wrong."

"Well, I'd rather bear my own cross if that's the case," Kate says sadly, wiping a lock of hair from her face.

Then, the school bell rings in the distance.

"It's time," Kate says. "Daisy and Bobby, let's go!"

The four of us head out. Daisy walks between Kate and me, swinging our arms back and forth until her mother tells her to stop because her arms are getting sore. Bobby runs ahead of us. Fortunately, my shoes have dried out quite well. Paul had heated stones in the fire last night and placed them in our shoes, wrapped in cloth. I'll need to do that again when we get home. Every time I go outside, my shoes get wet from the sticky snow.

Chattering excitedly about the new school, Daisy walks next to me. She must be nervous about her first day. As we chat, we arrive in the village. It's bustling with activity.

I see the pub where we met Dylan last night. Among several other buildings, I spot two hotels, a church, a horse stable with a blacksmith, and a store.

The refined gentleman, whom I saw yesterday with the ladies, comes out of one of the buildings. Paul also emerges from the small building behind him.

He has a notebook and pen in hand, clearly planning to extract some information from the mine director. It doesn't seem like the director will readily divulge his mining secrets to a curious journalist. They don't notice us, and we continue to the church, which also serves as the school building. Various children are milling around the church, and I see that we have five minutes before classes begin. In the distance, a few children are running up, apparently trying not to be late.

"Good morning," the teacher greets us, standing by the church door.

A low gate separating the schoolyard from the road is wide open, and we walk up to him.

"Good morning," we reply.

The teacher is a tall, slender man in his mid-thirties, slightly older than I am. He wears a hat, so I can't see the colour of his hair, but I suspect he's blonde. His beard is definitely that colour.

Kate introduces herself and the children to the teacher, and he shakes both their hands.

"Welcome," he says.

"Do you have a seat available for them in your class?" Kate asks.

"It's quite full, but it should work," says the teacher.

Bobby tugs at Kate's hand. "Can I go play now?" he asks.

Kate lets him go, and he runs into the yard. Daisy follows, but much more calmly than her wild little brother.

"I heard from my aunt that you are her neighbour," I begin politely, starting a conversation.

The teacher looks at me in surprise. "Are you from Victoria?" he asks, matching my politeness.

"No," I say. "We're from Vancouver. My aunt, who lives in Victoria, was with us over Christmas, and we traveled to the island together. She told me that her neighbour is the teacher at the school in the village on Mount Sicker, and I'm assuming that's you."

"Well," he says with a laugh, "there's only one school here and one teacher, so she must have meant me."

I also laugh, relieved that I haven't made a mistake by addressing the wrong teacher.

"How does it work," I ask with interest, "with all ages in one class? That must be quite a challenge."

"It certainly is," he admits. "It would be nice if the village committee would approve another teacher. It would make the classroom more peaceful and also save a lot of grading work. Unfortunately, I haven't been able to find a suitable candidate yet."

Before I can stop myself, I blurt out, "I'm a teacher myself. Maybe I can help you with something while I'm here."

Then the school bell rings again, and the children run to the front door, where they line up neatly.

"That sounds good," says the teacher. "Come by when you have time."

"I'll do that," I say. "Goodbye, Teacher…"

"You can call me Jelle. And what is your name?"

"I'm Elsa. Feel free to use 'you.'"

He smiles and tips his hat slightly. "Goodbye, Elsa. Goodbye, Kate. See you later."

I thought so. He has blonde hair.

"See you later," we both say.

As we walk away, Kate warns, "It's fine that you're going to help at the school, but don't forget that you're only here temporarily. Know what you're getting into. Who would want to live here on this mountain, in this filthy blackness?"

I shrug. "Who's talking about staying here? I told the teacher that I can help while I'm here." I give her an arm. "Don't worry, Kate."

We do some shopping at the grocer and walk back to the tent. The sun has broken through the grey clouds and shines on the snow. We can now look over the entire valley and see to the south, just over the border with America, the snow-covered Mount Baker. Closer, we see the water in the bay at Cowichan Bay. As far as we can see, smoke rises from the tipis of the First Nations people and the few farms of the English.

At noon, the children come running home for their lunch of beans with bacon, which we eat around the fire pit in the middle of the tent. Daisy and Bobby are both excited about their new school.

Shortly after I hear the steam whistle at the end of the afternoon, Dylan comes home. "Is there food? I'm starving," he complains as he walks in without greeting. His face is smeared with soot from working in the mine.

"The food is almost ready," says Kate hurriedly as she stirs the pot, she has taken off the fire. Above the fire hangs another kettle full of water being warmed so Dylan can wash.

"I'm a bit late," she apologizes.

"Couldn't you start cooking earlier?" Dylan grumbles. "You know I'm hungry when I get home. I've been working hard all day. I'm tired."

"We're all hungry, and we've all done what we needed to do," Kate retorts. "We took Daisy and Bobby to school, did the shopping and the laundry, and cooked the food," she defends herself.

Dylan snorts disdainfully. An angry light burns in his eyes. "You'd better go look for work tomorrow," he says roughly to Kate. "We can use every penny until we make a big find on our land."

Kate nods hesitantly.

I grab a stack of plates and set them on the small table next to the fire, which serves as a countertop.

Then Paul enters the tent. "Good evening, everyone," he says cheerfully. "I hope I'm not too late for dinner. Or is there not enough for an extra person?" he asks Kate. Seeing

Dylan's face, he adds, "Don't worry, I'll pay for it if you want."

Although I suspect Dylan would be fine with that, he nods for Paul to join.

Kate serves the plates as everyone sits around the fire. Paul asks the children with interest how school went while Dylan looks at him as if he'd like to throw him out of the tent. I'm grateful to Paul for at least paying attention to the children — attention they don't get from their father but also don't ask for.

"I have a new friend," Daisy says. "Her name is Amber, and she lives in the hotel."

"Then she must have wealthy parents," Dylan suddenly asks with interest.

"No," says Daisy. "She lives there with her mother. Her mother works in the hotel."

"What kind of work does she do there?" Kate asks with interest.

"I'm not sure. Amber called it 'entertaining the customers.'"

We look at each other.

"Okay," Dylan says slowly, "just make sure to stay away from that hotel."

Daisy looks at him, confused. "Can't I go play with Amber after school?"

"No," says Dylan. "You can't. It's better if you find another friend."

Tears well up in Daisy's eyes.

"Bring Amber here sometime," Kate says comfortingly. "She can come play with us."

Daisy looks from Kate to Dylan.

Dylan looks back, resentful, but says nothing more.

❧

The next morning, we take the children to school again. Afterward, we plan to stop by the grocer to see if he might know of any work for Kate.

The teacher greets us as we drop off the children at the gate. At the same time, a woman arrives with a girl by her side. As soon as the child sees Daisy, she runs up to her.

"Mama," says Daisy, pulling at Kate's sleeve, "this is Amber."

Kate smiles at her, and Daisy and Amber head off together into the playground.

The woman stands next to us. "Hello," she says.

We greet the elaborately dressed woman somewhat cautiously.

The teacher comes over to us, and Kate seizes the opportunity to ask if he knows where she might find work.

"I'll keep my ears open," he says. Then, the schoolchildren call for his attention.

"Excuse me," says Amber's mother, "I couldn't help but overhear your conversation with the teacher, but there's a job available at our hotel."

"Oh no," says Kate, alarmed. "I'm not going to work there. Not a chance."

"But," Amber's mother says hesitantly, "it's work you can do indoors, in the warmth of the hotel."

"No," Kate says again, "what makes you think I'd want to do that kind of work?" she asks angrily.

"Well," the woman continues, "it pays well, you'll be inside, you can have lunch with the staff, and you can go home when the mine whistle blows."

"But," Kate says suspiciously, "I thought you mostly worked in the evenings when the men come out of the mine."

"That's true, but the laundry and mending can be done during the day."

For a moment, Kate is left speechless. "Sorry," she says, embarrassed. "I thought you were offering me a job similar to yours."

"Oh no, no," says Amber's mother with a relieved laugh. "That's not what I meant. Our laundress is going to work in Duncan, and we haven't found anyone to replace her yet."

Then we all laugh heartily, and I'm glad that Kate can laugh about it, too.

"Come by later," says the woman. "The cook will be in the kitchen. Ask her about the job; I'll tell her you're coming by."

"Thank you," says Kate. "I'll come by shortly." She hesitates for a moment, then asks, "Would you like to come for lunch with us?"

Amber's mother's eyes light up. "Yes, I'd like that."

"What's your name, by the way?" I ask her.

"My name is Olga," she says.

"Are you from Russia?" I ask, intrigued by her accent.

She nods.

"Why did you come here?" I ask curiously. "Russia is a prosperous country with a good economy, isn't it?"

Olga shakes her head. "It only seems that way. Russia is far behind Europe. It is a powerful country with nearly two million soldiers, but we had many problems after the Crimean War ended in 1856. Factory workers went on strike for better working conditions, and there was much political unrest. I worked fifteen hours a day in a newly opened factory. After Amber was born, I decided to leave Russia with a friend and her husband."

"And Amber's father?" I ask cautiously.

"I don't know who Amber's father is," says Olga with a shrug.

"I'm sorry," I say, not knowing what else to say.

A little later, we knock on the back door of the Brenton Hotel.

"Good morning," says the cook gruffly, stirring a pot on the stove.

"I'm here for the job Olga told me about," Kate says.

"Then you must be Kate?" she asks. "I could use some extra help now that that girl left early yesterday morning. She found it an un-Christian place here. She didn't know the hotel offered special female services to men. Can you believe that?" The cook says disdainfully. "Aren't you put off by the work the women here do?" she asks, casting a wary look at Kate.

"You don't have to take the job," I say softly to Kate. "You can find your own clients if necessary."

"That's true," says Kate. She thinks for a moment. "Tell me," she says, turning to the cook. "How much does it pay?"

The cook mentions the amount, and I can see from Kate's face that it's much more than she expected.

"For how many days a week?" she asks.

"Monday through Thursday. By Friday, everything needs to be washed, ironed, and repaired. Weekends are the busiest time for the other staff, but you don't need to be here then."

"Okay," says Kate. "I'll take it."

"Great," says the cook, and a rare smile appears on the weathered face of the kitchen general. "Come tomorrow to start on the backlog of work left by that deserter."

After lunch, once the children are back at school and Olga has returned to the hotel, we sweep the tent, do the laundry, and prepare dinner. We have a cup of tea, and then we hear the children approaching on the path. A little later, the steam whistle sounds, and Dylan comes home.

"I'm starting work at the hotel tomorrow, doing the laundry and mending," Kate tells Dylan as we all sit around the fire with bowls of hot food in our hands.

To my surprise, Dylan nods approvingly. He doesn't mention the activities at the hotel. Or perhaps he thinks Kate has found a job at the other hotel, the posh Mount Sicker Hotel?

The next morning, after breakfast, Kate and the children head to the village for work and school. I wave them off and wish Kate good luck with her new job. After tidying up the tent, I decide to explore the surroundings. Maybe I can find herbs to use in cooking or for making salves and tinctures.

There's too much snow up on the mountain, so I walk down the path. Gradually, the snow cover thins out until there's no snow halfway down the mountain. I have to stop frequently as heavily loaded wagons rumble past me on their way to the train that will carry the ore to the smelter in Crofton.

I find only some old mint leaves from the previous season, which I can use to make mint sauce. Maybe I can give apple vinegar an extra flavor with mint and peppercorns. Lost in thoughts of recipes, I almost reach the bottom of the mountain. I greet an elderly First Nations woman who, like me, is searching for herbs along the roadside.

It's time to head back so I can make it in time for lunch.

I have barely returned to the tent when I see Daisy and Amber skipping toward me in the distance. Behind them walk Paul and Kate. Bobby is running around them.

That boy, I think, might fall and rip another hole in his pants and knee.

At that moment, a rumbling shakes the ground, reverberating from deep inside the mountain. A chilling silence follows, hanging momentarily in the crisp air.

A siren begins to wail, and women rush out of the tents and houses in the village. I see Paul and Kate turn around and run back toward the village.

I need to go too, I think, anxious and panicked. The men are still in the mine! The steam whistle of the mine, which signals lunchtime, has not yet sounded.

I gather my skirts and start running toward the village. There's chaos everywhere. Everyone is rushing toward the mine entrance. The miners' wives are frantically searching for their husbands, who have gathered at the entrance. I see tears of relief on the faces of those who have found each other. Kate is also nervously weaving through the crowd. I follow closely behind her.

"Have you seen my husband, Dylan?" she asks a few miners.

They shake their heads. "We think there are still a few inside."

Kate's eyes widen in fear. She puts her hand over her mouth.

The dignified gentleman, the mine director, is giving orders. "Step back!" he calls. "Everyone must stay away from the entrance. The mine entrance has collapsed due to a gas explosion."

It soon becomes clear that three men are missing. The names Dylan, Fred, and Henry are mentioned. Kate continues to search in vain among the men at the entrance, who are now entering the mine with wheelbarrows to clear the collapsed tunnel.

"Come," I say to Kate, "let's sit down for a moment."

I point to a few snow-covered logs and start clearing a patch of snow with my sleeve. "There's nothing we can do right now except wait."

Shivering, we sit on the logs and watch the men going in and out of the mine with wheelbarrows. Olga comes over and brings us a cup of hot tea and some food. It's already getting dusky in the early afternoon. Soon, it will be very dark.

Olga suggests going to the pub to warm up. "Daisy and Bobby are there with Amber," she says when she sees Kate hesitating.

"Come on," I say, "let's wait in the pub until the tunnel is cleared."

I tell a miner where we'll be. He smirks at Kate. "Her husband's late home once, and she heads straight for the pub."

I'm so stressed by the events of the past days that I give him a sharp slap across his grimy face for this inappropriate joke. Immediately, I'm startled by my own reaction. I step back and stammer an apology.

The white eyes in the black face of the man stare at me, and for a moment, I'm afraid I'll get a slap in return. But then, to my surprise, he apologizes.

"It's okay," I say wearily.

Then I follow Kate and Olga to the pub.

After sitting outside for hours in the cold wind, we are both chilled to the bone.

Inside the pub, we find a seat near the fire. Daisy, Bobby, and Amber come over to join us. Paul, who is also at the pub, worriedly asks if we have any updates and brings us blankets, draping them over our shoulders.

I feel the pitying glances of the men in the pub. Everyone is shocked by the mine accident. At the table next to ours, a grimy man is trying to persuade his companions to play a card game. I see them shaking their heads, stealing glances in our direction. At a table farther away, they finally start a game. The further removed you are from the situation, the quicker you forget the suffering of others, I think bitterly.

Kate stares ahead, her red hands clasped around a hot cup of tea. "What if they're not alive anymore?" she asks, her voice heavy with dread.

"Let's not jump ahead of the story," I try to divert her from the worst thoughts. "We don't know anything yet about the three men in the mine or what the situation really is."

"You know," she says suddenly, intensely, "I don't care if something's happened to Fred, but I don't want to lose Dylan."

"Kate," I say, startled, "you shouldn't talk like that." I glance around nervously to see if anyone has overheard her.

"Elsa," she snaps angrily, "you don't know what I've been through."

"That's true," I admit, "I only have a vague idea."

The image of Dylan in the pub on the night we arrived in the village flashes into my mind. I see us all trudging behind him through the snow while he storms ahead, angry and smoking. I picture the pile of wood behind the tent that he still hasn't used to build a house, even though he knew Kate and the children were coming after Christmas.

"Come on," I say as I lean forward and take her hands. "Let's pray." I lay the whole situation before God, trusting He'll hear us.

"Thank you," Kate whispers as we open our eyes again. Her voice is discouraged. "Do you think He can hear us?"

"You must not doubt that. You know He hears us," I reply gently. "Negative thoughts just lead you into a downward spiral—you don't want to go there."

"I'm already there," she sighs sadly.

"Cheer up," I try to comfort her, but my words sound hollow even to me.

Then I fall silent. What if the three men are dead? What does that even mean? What's the point? How will Kate and the children manage without Dylan? What about the debt on the land he bought? Pa isn't wealthy enough to cover that. My teaching job barely covers my own room and board, let alone allowing me to help Kate financially.

Then, the thought of wealthy Aunt Margaret crosses my mind, but I dismiss it immediately.

Kate would never accept help from her. Aunt Margaret condemned the entire gold-seeking venture when she heard about Kate's plan to go to Mount Sicker.

"Gold fever," she had said, "is something people with short-term plans have. You need to have a plan for the future and not jump from one possibility to another. It's like getting on a train, changing your mind, and switching to a train with a seemingly better destination. You never get anywhere that way. That's what you're doing. You're just hoping for luck," she had said. Yet Kate had gone. After all, she saw no other option but to follow her husband.

I'm jolted out of my thoughts when the pub door is thrown open.

"We've made contact," shouts the miner standing in the doorway.

Everyone stands up and follows the messenger outside into the icy cold night.

"We hear knocking," he explains.

"They're still alive!" I give Kate a nudge.

She starts crying and laughing through her tears.

We head back to the mine entrance. Miners are still coming out of the mine with wheelbarrows full of debris.

Shivering from the cold, we stand at the entrance to the mine. The wind blows through our thin coats.

A little later, the messenger comes back to us. "You'd better go back into the pub," he says. "It will probably take a while. I just wanted to let you know that we're making progress. I'll come back when I know more. I'm going to alert the doctor and tell her that they might be injured and need help."

"Oh, dear," Kate sobs. "What if they're alive, but Dylan is so injured that he can never work again? How will I manage on my own?"

I pull her close. "Don't think about that yet. Remember what Grandma always said? A person often suffers more from the suffering they fear. Let's not worry about things we don't know yet."

"Yes, but," she starts again, "what if..."

"Shh," I say soothingly. "Let's just wait and see."

We return to the pub. The hour that follows drags by like a snail.

Then the messenger comes back in. He heads straight for us.

"We have an opening," he says.

Kate jumps up.

"Wait a minute," he says. "I should mention that your husband is injured. He won't be able to walk out of the tunnel by himself, and we're taking measures to carry him out on a stretcher. The opening needs to be large enough before he can be brought out."

Kate is beside herself with nerves. I follow her out into the freezing cold behind the messenger. Apparently, the news has already spread through the village, even at this late hour. People are gathering, curious about how this will turn out. Everyone carries a lantern, and if you didn't know better, you'd think it was a festive winter procession.

I see a couple of men constructing a stretcher in front of the mine entrance.

"The stretcher can come in," someone calls from inside the mountain.

The men hammer in the final nails. While two of them pick up the handles on either side, someone quickly throws a quilt onto the stretcher before the bearers disappear into the mine.

Kate and I huddle together, shivering. The wind howls through our coats and makes our skirts flutter. We wrap our shawls around our heads. Drizzly snowflakes lash against our faces.

The doctor, who, to my surprise, is the old First Nations woman I met this morning during my herb search, has gone inside with them. We anxiously await the moment when the bearers will come back out.

Behind us, the crowd of spectators grows. The lanterns give off some warmth, and since everyone is standing close together, the cold is not so biting anymore.

"Move aside, move aside," calls a miner who comes out of the mine, holding his lantern in front of the bearers.

Kate and I ignore his shouting. We move forward and walk closely beside the stretcher. Kate grabs Dylan's hand. His eyes are closed. His face looks pale against the soot stains.

The procession heads toward the pub. In the middle of the tavern, a few men make space by moving some tables. The scraping sound of the table legs against the wooden floor is painful to my ears.

The First Nations doctor, wrapped in a beige blanket adorned with images of mountain lions and bears, sets down a bag of supplies and medicine on the floor and kneels beside the stretcher. Kate and I kneel on the other side. Daisy, who had fallen asleep earlier in the evening with Bobby wakes up due to the commotion. She wriggles between us.

"Dad," she calls, "Dad, wake up!"

Dylan doesn't move.

I pull Daisy close to me. "Let the medicine woman take a look first," I say soothingly. "We can speak to him later."

"Is he dead?" she asks anxiously.

"No," I say, "he's not dead."

"Is he going to die?" she asks again.

Bobby has also woken up. With wide, frightened eyes, he looks at the scene. He comes to stand next to me. I put an arm around both children and hold them close. My legs are aching from kneeling, but I don't move.

Fred has also come to stand nearby. At a distance, I see Henry, the man they pointed out as being in the mine as well. He is a tall, skinny man with a brown cowboy hat. He looks grim. Fred and Henry came out relatively unscathed, unlike Dylan. I stare at my brother-in-law's face.

Then I stand up and move the children over to Paul, who is sitting next to the stretcher. I walk toward Henry. For a moment, it seems like he might try to walk away, but then he straightens his back and looks at me challengingly with his sharp eyes.

"What exactly happened in the mine?" I ask him.

"The tunnel collapsed," he says curtly.

"How come," I ask further, "you couldn't reach the exit in time while the other miners did?"

"Those two," he says angrily, "were arguing. They didn't listen to the knockers who were warning us. I couldn't get them separated in time. Those fools," he mutters irately.

"Knockers?" I ask, puzzled. "Who are they?"

"Little creatures that live in the mines," Henry says stiffly. "Just before the walls of the mine shaft collapse, they knock on the walls to warn us."

Seeing my confused look, he adds, "Believe what you want. The fact is, the walls collapsed after I and others heard the knocking."

I don't know how to respond to this.

"What were they arguing about?" I ask.

"That's none of my business," he snaps. "I don't want to get involved. One thing I will say: be careful with Fred; he's crazy."

I turn my head toward the group around the stretcher and see Fred pacing nervously, constantly trying to view the situation from different angles.

Strange behaviour, indeed.

When I turn back, I see that Henry has disappeared. I run to the door and peer into the dark night but can't see him anywhere.

Then, I slowly return to the stretcher and look down at my brother-in-law. He is restlessly moving his head. The First Nation doctor has cut open his shirt and is cleaning a severe shoulder wound. Now that Dylan has turned his head, I see he also has a head wound.

I attempt to speak to Fred. "What exactly happened in the mine?" I ask cautiously.

"The tunnel collapsed," he says.

I nod. "I heard that. We heard the explosion," I continue. "Why couldn't you reach the entrance in time?"

"We just didn't," he says gruffly, "because of the explosion, the tunnel collapsed, and the rocks blocked the way to the entrance."

These answers aren't getting me anywhere. I don't want to irritate him further, so I remain silent. Still, I want to find out if their argument really caused the delay that prevented them from reaching the entrance in time. I walk a bit away from Fred and approach a young man I recognize from the ride from the train to the mountain village.

"Who else was in Fred's and my brother-in-law's mining group?" I ask him.

"Me and my buddy here," he points out.

"Why couldn't they leave in time, but you could?"

For a moment, their eyes, hidden beneath their black faces, stare at me. Then the young man says, "Fred and Dylan were arguing and weren't moving fast enough. I heard Henry shouting that they had to hurry and go straight to the exit, but then the explosion happened. The explosion was right behind us. We were both thrown to the ground by the blast," he says, showing me his scraped hands, "but we managed to get away."

"What were they arguing about?" I ask.

"That's not my concern, Miss," he says. "I don't want any trouble with Fred. Ask him yourself; he's a friend of yours, right?"

I make a face of disdain, signaling that I don't consider him a friend. "Thank you," I say and turn back to the group on the ground.

The medicine woman has bandaged the wound, and Dylan is now conscious. He groans. Kate is sitting next to him on the floor, holding his hand. Fred is still pacing back and forth. I'll have to wait until Dylan is a bit more coherent and able to answer questions.

Slowly, the pub becomes emptier. Most people have gone home to sleep for a few more hours before the whistle blows and everyone has to get up again. The mine entrance needs to be cleared and the walls supported. Work must continue. The sun is cautiously rising above the mountains on the other side, tinting the sky a soft pink. Not long after, the village comes back to life.

"We'll carry you home," say a few miners who come back into the pub after a very short night, speaking to Dylan.

They pick up the stretcher after we've covered Dylan with extra blankets. Maneuvering between the tables, they head out the door. Kate walks with them.

I gently shake Daisy and Bobby's shoulders, who have fallen asleep next to the hearth. They scramble upright, looking around bewildered.

Then they remember where they are. "How is Dad?" they ask.

"The doctor has cleaned his wounds, and now he needs to heal. They're going to take him home. Come on, let's go," I say and take Daisy's hand. Bobby runs ahead of us to the door.

Paul is still sleeping with his head on his arms at a table. He'll find his way home on his own.

"Thank you," I say to the landlord.

He waves it away with the dishcloth draped over his shoulder. "I hope he gets better."

"I hope so, too," I say, and I mean it. I just hope he's learned his lesson and won't squander his life or drown it in booze again.

We walk together across the frozen snow to the tent. When we arrive, Kate is already busy lighting the fire. It is just as cold inside as it is outside. The men who carried the stretcher leave.

Kate thanks the bearers and closes the tent door behind them.

Dylan lies quietly with his eyes closed on his bed. The medicine woman sits next to him.

"She gave him something to drink," Kate says softly when I ask. "He'll probably sleep for a while."

"It smells strange in here," I say.

"The medicine woman threw some juniper in the fire. It's to ward off evil spirits," Kate says.

"Kate," I say, alarmed, "you didn't let her do that, did you? You don't really believe in that, do you?"

"No, I don't believe in it either," Kate says softly, "but she asked me to throw it in the fire, so I did."

I shake my head disapprovingly. "What else did the doctor do?"

"She made a paste from the dogwood bark and applied it to the wounds. That should help."

I nod. The dogwood tree grows abundantly here, and the First Nations use the inner bark to treat various ailments.

Not long after, Paul enters the tent to check on Dylan. "Is there anything I can do for you?"

"I don't know," says Kate, looking visibly exhausted.

"Could you perhaps go to Duncan and call our parents and Dylan's?" I ask.

"I'll do that," Paul says. "Should I bring anything from Duncan?"

We can't think of anything, and Paul leaves. Not long after, I see him driving down the mountain with the grocer's horse and wagon.

৯৹৫

"Your mother was shocked," Paul says as he comes back into the tent around lunchtime. "Your father wasn't home, so I didn't speak to him. Rose took the phone from your mother.

In her impulsiveness, she wanted to come here immediately. I talked her out of it."

"Oh, thank goodness," I say. "We can't feed more mouths at the moment. We also don't have enough space for everyone to sleep. And what would they even do here? Help us? With what?"

We eat something, and Kate tries to give Dylan some soup. He doesn't have much of an appetite. From his face, I can see he's in a lot of pain. He keeps drifting in and out of unconsciousness.

The worries don't lessen. Especially at night, Dylan is restless, and Kate has to keep getting up to help him. None of us are getting much sleep. Still, we try to maintain a routine. I drop the kids off at school in the morning. To get out for a bit, I also pick them up again at the end of the morning.

This time, no other mothers are waiting at school at lunchtime. In the distance, by the mine entrance, I see the train that comes to pick up the ore stop. The young driver jumps to the ground, and to my surprise, I see him helping two ladies out of the locomotive cab. With his soot-covered hands, he grabs their waists. I think to myself that there will probably be big black smudges on their dresses now. The ladies go into the grocery store. At that moment, the school door opens, and the children stream outside to go home for their lunch break.

"Aunt, Aunt!" Bobby calls to someone behind me. I turn around, and my eyes widen in shock. I see Rose and Jasmin coming toward us!

The girls give Bobby a big hug, and Daisy runs toward them as well.

"What on earth are you doing here?" I stammer. "Where are Mom and Dad?"

"We came on ahead," Jasmin says. "Mom was very shaken by the accident. They hope to come when Mom feels better."

Back in the tent, Kate also looks up in surprise. "What are you doing here?" she asks, annoyed.

"We're here to help you," Rose says.

Kate shakes her head in disbelief.

The girls crouch by Dylan's bed on the floor. "How is he?" they ask.

Dylan mumbles something unintelligible and groans.

"Come on," Kate says, "let him rest. He's in a lot of pain."

As we all sit around the fire and Kate serves tea, I look sternly at the twins. "Did Mom and Dad approve of you coming here without them?" I ask, still with disbelief in my voice.

"Yes," they both nod. "Dad put us on the ferry."

"But," I say, now really suspicious, "then you couldn't possibly be here so early in the day. When did he put you on the ferry?"

Rose and Jasmin look at each other. Then Rose casually says, "Oh, that was yesterday."

"What?" Kate exclaims in shock. "Where did you stay the night then?"

"On Salt Spring Island, at a black family's house," Rose says.

"Salt Spring?" I say, alarmed. "How on earth did you end up there? And look at your dresses—what have you been up to? Mom and Dad won't be happy to hear this, but you're

122

going to tell us everything. I hope nothing bad happened to you with all those men wandering around."

"Tsss, what do you think?" Rose says indignantly.

"I'll start with the phone call from Paul," Jasmin says and begins.

⧼∾⧽

Sarah knocked on the living room door.

"Come in," Mom called.

"Ma'am," Sarah said as she entered, "Paul is on the phone. He wants to speak to you or Mr."

Dad wasn't home, and Mom, who had been sitting in the large armchair by the fireplace, got up. Rose and I both stood and followed Mom to the hallway where the phone is.

"Hello," Mom said into the receiver.

Rose and I waited curiously for the news Paul had to share.

"Oh no," Mom said, and she sank into the chair next to the phone. "Oh no," she repeated. She let the receiver drop into her lap.

"What's wrong? What happened? What's wrong?" Rose urged.

When she saw that Mom wasn't able to continue the call, Rose picked up the receiver and said, "Hello."

After a moment of silence, she turned over her shoulder to me and said, "Dylan is seriously injured. A part of the mine collapsed, and Dylan and Fred were trapped. They were only freed after hours. Dylan has sustained severe wounds."

After some back-and-forth conversation with Paul, Rose put down the receiver.

Mom was in shock. Her hands trembled. "Why did they have to go to that terrible place?" she shivered. "Oh, girls," Mom said, wringing her hands nervously. "Oh, how terrible this must be for Kate and the children."

I helped Mom back to the armchair in the living room. She looked pale and fumbled nervously with her lace handkerchief. "Oh, what are we going to do now?" she lamented. "What will happen now with the girls and the children? Dylan was unconscious when they pulled him out of the mine. Just imagine—all that soot and dirt, and then completely unconscious…"

I saw Rose roll her eyes. Sarah brought some quick salt and let Mom smell it, then returned with a cup of chamomile tea. Mom calmed down a little.

"Paul promised to call me again if there's any change in Dylan's condition," Rose said. "He said the doctor has been by, and now he needs to recover."

"Now Kate has no husband to take care of her," Mom said nervously. "How will she manage on her own with the children?"

"Mom, just calm down. Elsa and Paul are there too," I said. "They'll help her with everything."

Mom covered her eyes with her hands and sobbed. "Oh, that poor child," she cried. "She has to go through so much. Always working hard and then with a husband who's so crippled. What has she gotten herself into?"

I see Kate frowning, but she doesn't say anything. Then Jasmin continues.

"Mom, just wait a bit longer to see what Paul says when he calls back," we tried to calm her.

Her lip trembled. "I knew it, I knew it," she said, crying. "What good can come from chasing gold!"

Rose and I stood there, somewhat stunned. We've never thought Dylan's plan was great either, but getting injured can happen anywhere. Just yesterday, someone was run over by a horse and wagon, not to mention the mail coach driver who was killed by a tree falling across the driver's seat during a storm. He was only 26 and just doing his job.

As soon as Dad came home, Mom started crying and complaining again. "Oh, Dad, what should we do? Should we go to them?"

"Calm down, we can't do anything," Dad replied. "There's a doctor looking after Dylan, and Paul is with the girls if there's anything that needs to be done that they can't do or don't know how to do."

Mom nodded and swallowed a sob. We sat at the table and poked at the food Sarah had served. After half an hour, with little eaten from the plates, we had her take them back to the kitchen.

"I'm going to lie down for a while," Mom moaned, disappearing through the door and slowly climbing up the stairs as if she had a heavy burden to carry.

Dad also got up and hurried after her. When he came back downstairs a little later, he said, "A bit of rest will do her good. Her nerves have had a severe shock."

"We're going," Rose said suddenly and resolutely.

Dad and I looked at each other with concern.

"What can we do there?" I said hesitantly.

"I'm going to pack my suitcase," Rose said and headed upstairs.

"That impulsive girl," Dad sighed.

"I'll go upstairs to Rose and try to talk her out of it," I said to Dad.

When I got upstairs, I also saw an open suitcase on my bed. It was still empty, unlike the suitcase on Rose's bed, which was almost packed.

"You need to pack your own suitcase," Rose commanded. "I'm not doing it for you."

For a moment, I stood there bewildered. I'm used to being bossed around, but this was a bit much. "Why do you always think you can boss me around?" I asked angrily.

Rose glanced at me sideways while she tossed a hairbrush and some ribbons into her suitcase. "Because otherwise, you wouldn't move. You just need a push to actually do something."

I felt exposed now that the truth was told to me so directly. It is indeed true that I always hope a problem will resolve itself, though I can't think of a time when it actually did.

Muttering to myself, I grabbed a dress and folded it before placing it in my suitcase.

"Good job, girl," Rose said.

Angrily, I said, "I have to come too because who will keep an eye on you with your reckless behaviour?"

As we went downstairs again, Dad reluctantly agreed that Rose and I should go to the island and that he and Mom would come later once Mom had calmed down and was able to travel.

"I still can't believe Dad agreed to let you come here. I'm not sure Mom will be able to make the trip later," I say.

Kate refills the mugs with tea and serves the plates for lunch. By now, Paul has also come into the tent and is just as surprised as we are to see the twins here.

"I thought," he says sternly to Rose, "that I told you not to come here."

Rose shrugs indifferently.

"Aunt Jasmin, tell us more. How did you end up on Salt Spring Island?" Bobby asks impatiently.

Jasmin takes a sip of her hot tea and continues her story.

Dad, Rose, and I went to the ferry in a rented Cadillac. Mom stayed home. She wasn't feeling well at all, so Sarah stayed with her.

It was the first time we would be riding in a car. Dad took the front seat next to the driver while Rose and I climbed into the back seat of the open carriage. We draped quilts over our knees and tied the scarves that were wrapped around our hats tightly under our chins. I had heard that it was supposed to be very windy due to the high speed of the vehicles. I had read that last summer, the Frenchman Victor Hémery, and the American Louis Chevrolet had broken the speed record by driving 110 miles per hour. I was convinced that this car wouldn't go that fast.

A drizzle of rain, falling from a grey, cloud-covered sky, streaked our faces as the car picked up speed. By the time we arrived at Burrard Inlet, where the ferry was waiting, our coats were soaked through.

127

Shivering, we got out. The driver helped Dad with our suitcases. The gangway was already out, and Dad walked with us to the boat. We hugged each other.

"Be careful, girls," Dad said.

"Of course," I smiled, trying to brush off his concern, but deep down, I was nervous about the unknown we were heading into. Paul's stories about the Klondike kept echoing in my mind.

We picked up our suitcases and made our way to the gangway.

"Come here, girls," Dad said, and he pulled us both to him for another hug. He held us tightly as if it were the last time he would see us alive.

"Well," I say, "do you think it's strange he feels that way, with all the trouble you've caused over the years?"

Rose snorts. "It's not that bad," she grumbles.

"And then?" Bobby asks. "What happened next?"

Jasmin smiles and runs her hand through his hair. She continues.

৩৹৵৩

When the Cadillac, with the driver and Dad in it, turned the corner, an announcement came from the captain. The boat's engine was broken, and it might take a few hours to fix. Everyone was asked to wait calmly.

After ten minutes, Rose's patience wore thin. "We're going to find another boat," she said.

I was startled. "Where do you think you'll find one?"

Rose looked over the railing and saw a few First Nations people talking by their canoes a little farther off.

"We'll ask those men," she decided.

Along with a few other passengers who were strolling on the dock while waiting for the boat to be repaired, she went down the gangway. Rose headed straight for the First Nations men. I had no choice but to trot after her, dragging our suitcases with me.

The First Nations men looked up when Rose arrived. One of them was wearing a grey sweater with a brown bear knitted into it; the other had the same sweater but with an eagle on it.

"The ferry is broken," Rose said. "Will you take us across?"

The men looked at each other. Then they nodded.

"How much?" Rose asked.

The First Nations man thought for a moment and named a price. Rose dug into her purse and pulled out the money. She handed it to the man in the bear sweater. He helped with the suitcases and put them in the canoe. Rose also climbed in.

"Rose," I said anxiously, "what are you doing? Let's wait until the ferry is repaired."

"Jasmin, come on," Rose said in a tone that made it clear she wasn't going to change her mind. I had no choice but to step into the wobbly canoe as well.

Kate shakes her head. "Rose, Rose," she says. "You're incorrigible."

"Go on, Aunt Jasmin," Bobby says.

If the two First Nations men hadn't each held onto the canoe, Rose and I would have ended up in the water. The man in the bear sweater also climbed into the canoe.

"Are you coming too?" he asked the one in the eagle sweater.

He shrugged. "Okay," he said and climbed in last.

I clung nervously to the sides of the canoe. The First Nations men paddled, and we glided across the water.

"Where do you want to be dropped off?" asked the man in the bear sweater.

"We want to go to Mount Sicker," Rose replied.

"Then we'll go to Crofton," decided the man in the bear sweater. "We can also stop by Kuper Island to pick something up from our uncle."

The men rowed. They didn't say much, though they sang quite a bit. The repetitive "Hujehujehuje" started to get on my nerves.

After a few hours of rowing, we saw the ferry approaching in the distance.

"We could have waited just as well," I grumbled. "You and your fantastic ideas. My bum hurts from sitting on this hard bench, and I need to use the toilet."

"Alright, alright," said Bear Sweater. "We'll stop at Salt Spring Island so you can use the toilet."

The First Nations men headed straight for Salt Spring Island. Meanwhile, in the distance, we could see the ferry sailing past us, with people on the boat looking like tiny dolls walking around.

A few minutes later, the waves created by the ferry rolled in, crashing against the canoe and causing it to sway dangerously. I let out a shriek of fright.

Rose laughed at me. "Come on, don't be such a baby." The First Nations men paddled on unperturbed as if nothing was wrong. I clung to the sides of the canoe; my fear must have been written all over my face.

When the waves subsided, we approached a spot where the canoe could be pulled up on shore.

"Go ahead," Bear Sweater said.

Rose and I stepped out.

"But," I said anxiously, "there's no toilet here—not even an outhouse."

"Come on," said Rose, "they for sure mean we need to find a spot in the bushes."

Together, we walked into the foliage. Our skirts got caught on the blackberries.

"What if those First Nations men leave without us?" I said, worried.

"No way, why would they?" Rose asked.

We both looked for a place behind the bushes where we wouldn't be seen by the men.

When we were done, we straightened our skirts and climbed back over the rocks and through the thorny bushes, returning to the tiny beach. Rose led the way, holding the blackberry branches out of the way between two fingertips until I could take them over.

Suddenly, Rose ran down to the beach and shouted, "Come back, come back!"

The blackberry branch she had been holding slipped from her grip before I could take it. "Ouch!" The branch whipped across my face. Without thinking, I grabbed it. "Ouch." That hurt, too. I pushed the branch aside and ran down the slope to the beach.

Then, I saw the canoe drifting on the ocean. The First Nations men were rowing away without looking back. Our suitcases were left scattered on the beach.

Rose muttered under her breath. "Come back!" she shouted at the First Nations men.

"What do we do now?" I cried.

Even Rose didn't know what to do for a moment.

To the north, the beach soon ended in a rocky promontory that jutted far out into the water.

To the south, the beach extended a little farther.

"We'll go south," Rose decided. "I saw the ferry heading that way, between the islands to the west. The southern part of this island should be nearby. We'll try to walk around. There must be a dock—or maybe even a harbour—where the ferry or another boat can dock."

"I should have never listened to you," I grumbled. "You and your thoughtless ideas. First, you were too impatient to wait for the ferry to be repaired, and we should never have gone to the toilet at the same time."

"You know," Rose said, "complaining gets us nowhere. We're in this boat now, so we might as well make the best of it."

"Couldn't you use a different saying? I wish we had a boat," I complained.

"Come on," said Rose, "let's get moving. Be glad we still have our suitcases."

We picked up the suitcases and headed south. The beach consisted of large, smooth rocks. Sometimes, we had to jump to get to the next rock. Other times, we had to take a detour because of an inlet on the island and trudge through the foliage. Then, we tried to return to the beach and continued our journey. Again, we had to make another small detour when a pile of driftwood blocked our way. We scrambled over it and pressed on.

"Nice, isn't it," I sneered, "that we still have our suitcases?"

Rose wisely said nothing as we both dragged our suitcases over the slippery rocks.

"Oh no," Rose sighed as we reached the corner of an inlet that went deep inland.

"Now we have to go all the way around again. That'll take us at least an hour."

Exhausted, we sat down on the wet rocks.

"Isn't it better to wait for the tide to turn? Maybe we could just walk across," I suggested.

We stood up and checked how high the water normally came.

"It's not at its highest point yet," I sighed.

"And then it still has to go down," Rose added, irritated. "We're not waiting for that, are we?" She stood up and grabbed her suitcase to continue.

"Hey," I said, "do you hear that?"

"What? I don't hear anything," Rose said, annoyed.

"Be quiet. It's obvious you can't hear anything if you keep talking," I snapped.

We both stood still and listened. Then we both heard it. Not too far away, we heard mooing.

"Is that a cow?" we asked at the same time. We looked at each other with relief. Suddenly, we forgot our sore feet and torn skirts. Again, the cow mooed. The sound came from the end of the inlet. As if on command, we both quickened our pace.

Soon, the landscape changed. Instead of rocks, which we could relatively easily walk over, we were now in a dense forest. We wandered around a bit to find a path through the undergrowth. We dragged the suitcases through the thick foliage, climbed a steep slope, and then suddenly froze in shock.

A wild black dog jumped out of the bushes, barking ferociously. We froze in fear.

"What if that beast bites?" I whimpered.

Our fear intensified as we saw a large man approaching through the trees, his face as dark as his dog, with a rifle slung over his shoulder.

"Is… is that the devil or Bigfoot?" I asked anxiously.

"No, girl, get real," Rose hissed. "That's an African."

"I've… I've never seen one before," I stammered.

"Neither have I," whispered Rose.

"Hello, ladies," called the man in an American accent. That gave us a bit of courage.

"Hello," we said softly.

Rose began to babble. "We came from over there," she said, pointing vaguely in some direction behind us. "First Nations men left us behind on the beach and sailed away with the canoe. We've walked quite a long way. We're heading to Mount Sicker, where our sisters live."

"Mount Sicker," said the black man, surprised as he stopped in front of us. "You're on the wrong island. This is Salt Spring Island. Mount Sicker is across the water at Crofton."

"Can you show us the way to the ferry?" I asked timidly.

"Yes, I can," said the man, "but the ferry isn't running anymore today. It's getting late in the afternoon, but I can take you there early tomorrow morning."

We looked at each other, worried.

"Where will we stay when it gets dark? Are there bears and cougars on Salt Spring?"

The man nodded. "Come with me. You can stay at the farm tonight. Come on, Jack," he said to the dog. "We're going home."

The dog took off, and the man and we followed.

"Do you dare sleep at this man's farm?" I whispered to Rose as I wrestled my suitcase free from the branches it had caught on.

"Shh," she said. "He might hear you. We'll see what we do when we get there. There must be a path from his farm that leads to the harbour."

After ten minutes, we left the foliage behind and arrived at an open field. In the distance, we saw a log cabin. As we approached the field, passing a few curious cows and almost stepping in cow pies, we saw two black children emerge from the house. They ran toward us. Jack leaped around them as they neared each other. When they saw us, they shyly hid behind their father's long legs. We walked in a procession to the farm. A First Nations girl came out of the house with a large basket of laundry, which she set down by the river flowing past the house.

Next to the house, a black woman was stacking firewood under a shelter so it could dry. She looked up when she saw our group approaching. "Who have you brought now?" she asked her husband.

"I found them in the woods," he said. "First Nations men left the girls on the beach and sailed away."

The black woman shook her head. "Come inside," she said, leading us into the log cabin. "I'm Hanna, and this is Jeremy," she added, pointing to her husband.

"We're Rose and Jasmin," I said.

Inside the house, a pleasant fire was burning in the hearth. It looked very humble. We were given a cup of warm tea with milk, and the woman served us a piece of bread with cold meat.

"Thank you," we both said politely.

"They'll have to stay here tonight, then I'll take them to the ferry in Ganges tomorrow morning," Jeremy said.

He then went outside to chop more wood and put the cows in the barn for the night. As dusk approached and before it got completely dark, we made a bed of blankets in the cow shed behind the house with the First Nations girl.

The girl was pleased we were there.

"I have the same name as you," she said to Rose. "My name is Qel'qulhp."

We tried to pronounce her name, and after a few attempts, we managed quite well.

We told her about the canoe and the First Nations men who had abandoned us.

"There are indeed some First Nations people who aren't very good," she admitted. "But," she assured us, "most of them are good, although it's hard for us to forget the past and that our land was taken from us."

"Sorry," was all we could say, as we didn't know how to address such a large problem.

Before going to bed, we had dinner in the kitchen with the black family. The big, dark eyes of the little children stared at us across the table. Jeremy suggested calling Duncan tomorrow to let someone know about our journey to Mount Sicker.

"No," Rose and I said hurriedly. "That's not necessary. Tomorrow, we'll take the ferry and ask if someone can drive us from Crofton to the mountain. Our sisters would be worried. They have so much on their minds since our brother-in-law was injured in the mining accident."

"We heard about the accident," said Hanna. "Lord, have mercy on us," she prayed, looking up.

I had trouble sleeping that night. It was warm in the cow shed, but it smelled of cow dung, which I heard clattering on the ground several times. The hay was prickly. Mice scurried away, and a prowling cat meowed. In the distance, we heard the chanting and drums of a First Nations tribe. It sounded very monotonous, penetrating, and eerie.

In the morning, we thanked Hanna warmly and promised to write to Qel'qulhp.

The horse trotted cheerfully in front of the wagon we took to the ferry, and we arrived at Vesuvius Bay well in time. We thanked Jeremy, who immediately set off on the two-hour return trip. We sat on the dock. Once Jeremy had disappeared into the distance, there was no one else to be seen.

"Surely the ferry will come, right?" I wondered aloud, my voice full of uncertainty.

In the distance across the bay, we saw it lying there. A large plume of smoke was rising from the sawmill next to it. The wind was blowing our way, and we could smell the pungent wood pulp.

Behind us, we heard a horse and wagon approaching. We turned around and saw a woman in the driver's seat with three little children in the wagon, coming toward us.

We greeted her.

"Are you going to Duncan for shopping too?" she asked.

"We're going to Mount Sicker," we told her. "Our sisters are there. There was a mining accident, and our brother-in-law was injured."

"I've heard about the mine explosion," said the woman. "You can ride with me for a bit. There's still room in the wagon. On the way back, there won't be much space left with all the groceries I'm going to get."

"He's coming!" cheered one of the little boys in the wagon, pointing at the ferry across the bay, from which a plume of smoke was now rising. He danced up and down in the wagon.

"Sit down," his sister said, "or you might roll over the edge, and we'll have to take you straight to the doctor."

"Doctor?" the woman said. "There's no doctor in Duncan; he would have to come all the way from Victoria in case of an emergency. You'd better sit down on your bum," she added sternly. "I don't want any emergencies."

"There's no doctor in Duncan?" Rose asked the woman. "Who's been helping our brother-in-law, then?"

"That must have been a First Nations medicine woman. They know so much about herbs; he'll be in good hands."

I mused aloud, "Mom and Dad think we've already arrived safely, and our sisters don't even know we've left. Actually, no one is searching for us or worried about us."

"That's good," said Rose. "Then we don't have to explain what happened, and we won't get a reprimand from anyone."

138

"You got that wrong," I said a bit angrily to Rose. "Just wait until Dad hears your story."

"Why are you threatening us with Dad?" Rose said, now also angry. "He was okay with us coming here."

"Just calm down," Kate said. "Think about your brother-in-law."

Rose grumbled a bit more but let Jasmin continue.

When the ferry arrived, and one lone passenger disembarked, the woman's wagon with the children drove onto the ferry. Rose and I boarded on foot. Half an hour later, we stood on the shore in Crofton.

"That's the train going to Mount Sicker," the woman pointed to a heavy locomotive with carriages behind it. "You can choose: you can ride with me to the base of the mountain and climb the rest of the way up yourself, or you can ask if you can ride the train, which will take you all the way up."

That was an easy decision for Rose. "We'll take the train," she said. "Thank you very much for the offer, ma'am. Goodbye, children," she added and immediately started walking toward the smoking locomotive.

I had no choice but to follow Rose. I waved goodbye to the woman and children.

The woman looked at us somewhat pityingly. "It's your own choice," she called after us.

Rose didn't hear her. I looked back once more and shrugged, waving to the children as the woman set the wagon in motion.

The locomotive made a lot of noise, and a huge amount of steam billowed from it. A young man with a blackened face was shoveling coal into the hopper on top of the locomotive.

"Mister, mister," Rose called to him, "can we get a ride to the mountain?"

"What did you say?" he shouted back.

Rose repeated her question, but he still didn't hear her. He jumped down and walked toward us. "Ride with us?" he asked, surprised. "Such proper ladies want to ride with a steam locomotive covered in dirt and soot?" He laughed. Disbelief was clear on his face.

In the distance, I saw the woman and children turn the corner. That hope was now gone. Was this a good decision? I wasn't sure at all, and now I saw doubt on Rose's face as well.

"I'll ask the boss," said the young man. "Hey, boss," he called to an older man who was fiddling with one of the carriages behind the locomotive, "can these ladies ride with us to the mountain?"

The man stopped what he was doing and came over to us. He looked us up and down. "If these lovely ladies don't mind getting soot on their fine dresses and are okay with a cramped spot in the cab, then yes, you may ride with us. We'll be leaving in about ten minutes. Put your bags inside," he said, pointing to the door that led to the cab.

We looked anxiously at the steep black metal ladder on the side of the locomotive. It looked very narrow, as did the door.

"I'll help you with that," said the young man.

"Thank you," we said, relieved, as we watched him scramble up the ladder, carrying one of the suitcases with one hand and holding onto the railing with the other.

"Okay, ladies," the boss said once the two suitcases were safely in the cab. "Now it's your turn."

I caught a glimpse of a smirk on the boss's face as I glanced back.

"Look at how my dress looks now," I complained to Rose once we were finally in the cab.

I examined my skirt from all sides. It now had not only tears from the blackberries and wrinkles from sleeping in the cow shed but also soot stains from climbing up the dirty ladder. There was no place to sit, so we just stood around, looking out the window.

The boss inspected the connection between the carriages and the locomotive one last time, and then it was time to leave. After fiddling with the instruments, the young man pulled on a cord, and the steam whistle screeched through the clear morning air. I instinctively covered my ears.

Rose elbowed me. "Stop making a fuss."

Startled, I dropped my hands.

The train started moving. We left the grounds of the sawmill and smelter and headed toward Mount Richards, the first mountain we encountered from the bay. The train chugged along, zigzagging up the mountain.

"We won't stop at the top of Mount Richards," the boss explained. "There's been some prospecting for copper, gold, and silver, but so far, there hasn't been enough found to start a mine."

A few men jumped onto the train, wanting to ride to Mount Sicker. We went downhill into the valley, and ten minutes later, the climb began again.

"Our next stop is Mount Sicker," the boss said. "There, we'll load the wagons with ore from the mine and then bring it back to the smelter in Crofton."

"Thank you for letting us ride with you," I said, "and for not making us sit in the wagons like the other men."

"Haha," said the boss. "We might not look so tidy, but most of us had a good upbringing. What sets us apart from those who stay in the big cities is that we're adventurers. We can't stay in one place for too long."

Meanwhile, I peeked at the man's dirty clothes and rough hands.

After a slow climb up the mountain, during which we enjoyed the beautiful view over the valley, we stopped at the entrance of a mine. We got out of the locomotive while the young man, standing at the bottom of the ladder, took our luggage. He grabbed us around the waist with his black hands to help us down from the ladder. With a wide grin that showed his white teeth against his dark face, he wished us a good holiday. I looked at my waist with disgust, now streaked with more black smudges.

Rose laughed it off. "Girl, don't get upset. Once we're with Kate and Elsa, we'll wash our clothes, and everything will be fine."

We thanked the boss and the young man once more.

"And now?" I said. "Where do we find Kate and Elsa?"

We walked to the village and went into the general store to ask if they knew where our sisters lived. When we explained that we were here to help because Dylan had an accident in the mine, the storekeeper's wife immediately knew where we needed to go. She walked with us outside and pointed in the direction of the tents. "There's your sister's tent."

We walked toward the tents. My feet were aching, but fortunately, the end was in sight.

"Good grief," the storekeeper's wife sighed to her husband, who had come to stand beside her. "What a mess, more of those helpless girls on the mountain."

Rose turned around and called out, "I heard that!"

"And then," Jasmin says as she puts her arm around Bobby, "we saw you, Daisy, and Elsa by the school."

Kate and I exchange a meaningful glance. Will the twins ever truly mature?

In the meantime, Daisy and Bobby's lunch break is over. They must hurry to get back to school on time.

With Dylan sick, Kate can't go to the Brenton Hotel. Therefore, I pick up the mending and laundry from the hotel so we can work on it at home. When I return that afternoon, I see the twins scrubbing their dirty dresses in a large tub of soapy water outside the tent. Lacking a wringer, they use their hands to wring out the clothes. Kate has stoked the fire in the tent, and the twins hang the wet dresses beside it. It now smells just like home when Sarah does the laundry and hangs it up next to the stove in the kitchen.

In between household chores, Kate keeps checking on Dylan. He sleeps almost all day. She tries to give him some soup, but he has no appetite and complains about his head and neck.

143

"Hello," we hear someone calling from outside.

I go to check and see the medicine woman standing in front of the tent. I invite her inside. She kneels beside Dylan's bed and re-bandages his wounds with a paste made from dogwood. Dylan doesn't seem to notice her.

The next day is different. Dylan wakes up frequently. He has a headache, which could be a concussion. He grumbles, complains, and is irritable.

The medicine woman returns, this time bringing her granddaughter with her to learn how to use the medicines. They take a seat by Dylan's bed. When he opens his eyes, the medicine woman asks how he's feeling. He responds with a scowl.

Kate also comes to stand by the bed.

"Who's that?" Dylan asks Kate.

"This is the doctor," she says.

"I don't want that doctor," he replies.

"But," Kate says, "she's treated your wounds."

"You hear me," he says angrily. "I don't want her."

"I'm sorry," Kate says, embarrassed, to the First Nations woman.

The woman and the girl stand up. Without a word, they leave the tent.

Now Kate cleans the wound, washes the bandages, and puts fresh cloths on the injury. Despite her careful attention, she can't prevent Dylan's shoulder wound from festering the next day. Even the alcohol I buy for Kate at the pub doesn't seem to help. Dylan develops a high fever.

"I thought," I say on the fifth day Dylan has been in bed, "that Fred was his best friend, but I haven't seen him here yet."

"I thought so too," Kate says disdainfully. "Maybe that's why he hasn't been around? In times of trouble, you really get to know your friends, right?"

That afternoon, as we are plucking a chicken in front of the tent, Fred suddenly appears before us.

"I came to see how the patient is doing," he says as if Dylan has just caught a cold.

"He's in the tent in bed," Kate nods toward the tent entrance. "He has a fever, so don't stay too long, and don't tire him out."

"Don't worry, lady," Fred says dismissively.

Ugh, I think, what a nasty man. Fred nods at me and tips his hat. With tightly pressed lips, I nod back.

My thoughts drift back to an evening in Vancouver when I visited Kate and Dylan. Fred was there, too. It was time for Daisy and Bobby to go to bed, and Kate called them from the kitchen to come to her so they could get ready for the night.

"I'll just go get some more wood for the stove," Dylan said and disappeared from the living room.

I was then left alone with that oaf, who scrutinized me from head to toe.

"And how are you?" he asked with exaggerated interest.

"Fine," I replied, falling silent as I continued knitting a sweater for Daisy.

"No marriage plans yet?" he asked rudely.

"No, why would I?" I responded, irritated.

"Well," he said, "if no one asks you to marry them, you can always come to me."

"Whatever you think," I said sharply. "That will never happen." Immediately, I felt foolish for letting that unpleasant man get under my skin.

Fred laughed contemptuously.

Dylan re-entered with a stack of firewood on his arm and a block of wood in his hand. "How cozy in here," he said sarcastically.

"Pfff," I muttered, knitting furiously.

Luckily, Kate soon came into the room, and the mood lightened. I had always found Fred an annoying meddler, but since then, I can't stand him at all.

"I want to hear what Fred has to say," I say quietly to Kate.

"No, let them be," she replies. "Let them have their way."

"I haven't told Kate about the conversation I had with Henry and the young man in the pub. It would only add to her troubles. I want to find out if the young man's claims are true. Was it just a one-time argument, or has this been an ongoing issue that Kate and I don't know about?

I sneak to the side of the tent where I know Dylan's bed is.

"Hey, buddy, how's it going?" I hear Fred's loud voice.

A grumble is the response.

"Sooner or later, you'll have to talk about it, friend," Fred says. "But first," he adds in a friendlier tone, "you need to get better. I can't do anything with a sick friend."

Then I clearly hear Dylan say, "Get out of this tent. Go away. Hurry up! Just go!"

"Héhéhé, calm down, I'm leaving. I'll come back in a few days to check on you when you're feeling better. Go find your property papers and have them ready when I return."

I am startled. Has Dylan really gambled away his land? That can't be true!

I hurry back to the chicken and barely sit down before Fred exits the tent. He greets us cheerfully and arrogantly as if he's very confident of his position. I dare not tell Kate what I overheard.

❧

"Do you feel like taking a little walk?" I ask Paul that evening. The moon is shining, and the mountain is bathed in a clear blue light.

"That sounds good," Paul replies.

The children are already asleep. Rose is busy with a woodworking project, Jasmin is embroidering, and Kate is reading her Bible. We stroll down the path leading to the village, the snow crunching softly underfoot. Occasionally, I catch glimpses of deer darting away as we draw near.

"I want to tell you something," I say to Paul, "but you have to promise not to tell anyone."

"That sounds intriguing," he replies with a hint of a joke in his voice.

"No, I'm serious," I insist. "I don't want Kate to hear this. She has enough on her plate already, and maybe it's not as bad as it seems."

"Alright, tell me your story," Paul says. "I won't be writing any headlines about it."

I give him a mock, angry look, but when I see his kind face in the moonlight, I soften and begin telling him about the young man in the pub, about Henry, and the conversation I overheard. I also share Kate's suspicion that Dylan might owe Fred a debt, though she's not entirely sure. I tell him about the overheard discussion from that afternoon at the tent.

"It sounds like something is indeed wrong," Paul says. "Can you find out where that ownership document is? Maybe we should hide it until we know what's really going on."

"I think you're right," I agree. "As long as Dylan is sick and lying in bed, he won't be looking for it to give it to Fred. I think he'll postpone it as long as he can. I'll keep an eye out but won't mention it to Kate. She's got enough to deal with."

"That's true," Paul says. "But please don't try to solve their problems."

"Understood," I say. "But I can still help them, right?"

"Only if they ask for help; otherwise, you'll make it worse," Paul says.

In the meantime, I've linked my arm through his. It's difficult walking on the layer of frozen snow, which grows with each snowfall and melts a bit when the sun is at its highest, making the road dangerously slippery. We reach the village center, where a light is still on in the school.

"The teacher is probably grading homework or preparing for tomorrow," I say. Due to Dylan's accident, I haven't had the chance to assist the teacher, as I had suggested when we first met.

We stop when we hear beautiful music coming from the school.

"That sounds like a cello," Paul observes.

We listen for a while but soon start to shiver from the cold.

Suddenly, the music stops. We wait a moment, hoping a new piece will start, but when it doesn't, we turn to head back home. Just then, the school door opens behind us, and Teacher Jelle steps out, carrying his cello.

"Good evening," he greets us.

We turn around and return the greeting. I gesture toward the cello and say, "That sounded lovely. Do you play often at the school?"

"Yes," he replies. "My landlady isn't fond of music, so I come here to play."

"I thought it was wonderful," I say again.

Paul nods in agreement.

"Thank you," says Teacher Jelle. He points in the direction of his home and says, "It's getting late; I should head home. Tomorrow is another school day."

"Indeed," I agree, and we wish him a good night.

⚜

Paul holds the tent door open for me as we return. Kate is sitting beside Dylan's bed.

"How is he?" I whisper when I see that Dylan has his eyes closed.

"Not well, I'm afraid," Kate replies. "The medicine woman has to come again tomorrow morning. Dylan needs something for the fever urgently. The infection isn't improving. She can help him if he wasn't so stubborn," she says, both angry and sad.

I take Kate's place so she can get some rest in my bed. I stay awake long past midnight, watching over Dylan. When I can no longer keep my eyes open, I wake Kate, and we switch places. I collapse into a deep but brief sleep.

During breakfast, Dylan tosses restlessly in his bed. I get the children off to school and stop by the grocer to pick up some essentials.

"How is your brother-in-law?" the grocer asks as I'm about to pay.

"He has a fever, and the wound has gotten infected," I reply. "Dylan refuses to see the medicine woman."

"He shouldn't be so stubborn," the grocer says. "Those First Nations people know how to treat infections like that, but yes, as the saying goes, 'lie down with dogs, get up with fleas.'"

I glance at him, puzzled, and wait for more information.

"You know," the grocer continues impatiently, "Fred is a pompous, arrogant man who dislikes Indians. Dylan's probably picking up some of that attitude."

"What else can you tell me about Fred?" I ask.

"Fred? He's in league with that snooty mine owner. I wouldn't be shocked if there's more to this accident."

"What do you mean?" I ask cautiously. "What could be more to it? Fred and Dylan are friends, right?"

"Yes, but there's gossip about something valuable found on Dylan's land. Given Dylan's debt to Fred, I wouldn't be shocked if Fred is angling for a share."

"Debt to Fred? How did that come about?" I inquire, trying to mask my curiosity. At this point, I don't care that the grocer might be spreading rumors—I need to understand the situation.

"You're his sister-in-law, right? You, of all people, should know about his enormous gambling debts, right?"

My silence reveals my ignorance, and I feel embarrassed. My head starts spinning. I quickly pay for my groceries and head outside.

The school hasn't opened yet, and the children are playing in the playground. The teacher, with two girls on his arms, is making his way around the area. I need to talk to someone. I don't want to tell Kate—she'll start to panic. Paul is nowhere to be seen.

I stop by the playground gate. The teacher notices me and approaches.

"I need to talk to this lady for a moment," he tells the girls, directing them back to their play.

"I'm worried," I start, hesitating as I consider whether to reveal our family's troubles.

The teacher raises his eyebrows. "The children are doing well at school," he reassures me.

"No, no, it's not that," I clarify. "It's about Dylan."

"Is he not improving?" the teacher asks, now visibly concerned.

"No, he's not," I admit, as if that were the sole reason for my worries. "The fever won't break."

And then, I blurt out, "I just heard from the grocer that Dylan has significant gambling debts, and I'm afraid Kate will struggle to manage everything."

"I've heard about it," the teacher says, his face showing sadness. "It's a small world up here on the mountain."

Panic grips me. "What about Kate and the children? What can I do to help?"

The teacher looks at me, thinking it over. "It's a tough situation," he says with a sigh. "Let me think about it. I'll see what I can find out. If you come by tomorrow morning when you bring the children to school, I might have more information about the extent of the debt."

"Thank you," I say, feeling a wave of relief.

Suddenly, it feels as if the winter sun, shining brightly on the snow, is a bit warmer, and the reflection no longer stings my eyes. I conjure a smile, and for a moment, I trust him even more.

"I also told Paul about this," I say, then recount the conversation with Henry and the young man in the pub, as well as the exchange between Dylan and Fred that I overheard near the tent.

"It seems," says the teacher, "that we need to find out what really happened in the mine."

"Henry didn't want to talk to me," I say.

"Let me visit him," suggests Teacher Jelle. "Maybe he'll talk to me."

With a lighter heart, I walk back to the tent, but the relief is short-lived.

Kate stands wringing her hands by Dylan's bed. He tosses and turns, his face flushed and sweaty. The covers are thrown off, and his shirt is soaked with sweat.

"It's not going well at all," Kate says anxiously.

"I can go get the medicine woman," I suggest.

From the bed comes a low, rasping growl. "Don't do that," Dylan grumbles, "leave it alone."

I remain silent, glancing from Kate to my brother-in-law and back. Kate dabs Dylan's forehead with a cold, wet cloth once more. He seems to be losing consciousness but opens his eyes again a few minutes later.

That day, not much work gets done around the tent. Dylan is delirious, making strange noises. During lunch, we all sit silently by the stove. The children can't eat a bite, their eyes anxiously on their sick father.

Suddenly, Dylan sits up. Sweat pours down his forehead, and with wide, frightened eyes, he looks at Kate. "Stay away from Fred. He has no claim on our land, even though he says he does. It's all mine," he gasps, then collapses back onto the cushions. Wearily, he closes his eyes, but they snap open again. "Do you hear what I'm saying?" he says hoarsely. "Not a single cent belongs to Fred."

I glance at Kate sympathetically. She jerks to her feet, but I don't mention the debt Dylan seems to owe Fred, according to the villagers.

Just before dinner, I follow Paul outside. I tell him that Teacher Jelle has promised to talk to Henry.

At that moment, we hear shouting not far from us. "What's that?" I ask, alarmed.

It's getting dark, and Paul says, "I'm going to check it out."

"Be careful," I urge him.

Paul heads toward the tents, which are situated a bit farther away. Most of the vegetation has been cleared, but the landowners have left some bushes and a few trees scattered here and there. I follow Paul slowly, struggling to climb the uneven ground. Kate and Dylan's tent is located along the

152

accessible path leading to the village, but higher up, there are also tents and makeshift houses spread out.

As we approach one of these houses, we spot Henry standing in the doorway. Fred is a few meters away. To my horror, Henry is waving a hunting rifle.

Paul and I duck behind a bush.

"Get out of here!" Henry shouts at Fred.

Slowly, Fred retreats and heads back to his tent.

Paul and I stay hidden behind the bush until Fred is safely inside his tent.

"Should I talk to Henry?" Paul suggests.

"I don't think this is the right time. He's too angry. Besides, the teacher is going to visit him tomorrow," I say, still unsure of how to handle the situation.

We return to the tent and eat our dinner in silence. Then, through the darkness, we hear the sound of a horse and wagon approaching. Paul gets up and steps outside. I follow him, standing by the tent door, trying to see who is passing by so late. The wagon is already too far away for me to make out the driver's face.

Paul starts running after it.

The wagon doesn't stop. I hear Paul's voice calling out, and then, in the dim light from the lanterns hanging from the wagon, I see the driver lash out with a whip, striking Paul hard. Paul lets out a cry. The wagon continues on, leaving Paul standing alone. I watch as it disappears down the road, vanishing behind the trees.

Paul comes walking back toward me.

"Who was that?" I ask, worried.

"Henry," Paul replies, his voice laced with anger. "He hit my hand."

We go inside the tent, and under the firelight and the glow of the lanterns, I see a thick, nasty stripe across Paul's hand, with blood oozing from the wound.

"It'll be fine," he says suddenly, trying to sound light-hearted, as though he's already forgotten the whole incident. He licks the blood off his hand, acting as though it doesn't hurt.

"I wonder why that jerk disappeared all of a sudden," Paul mutters.

"What jerk?" Dylan asks. He seems to have a moment of clarity.

"Henry," Paul replies.

"Henry is gone?" Dylan asks. "Makes sense," he then says. "Fred is making his life miserable."

"Why?" I ask.

"Fred thinks everything belongs to him, but that's not true." Then Dylan falls silent and drifts away again.

"The fever is rising again," Kate says worriedly a little later. She tries to give Dylan some of the remaining tea from the medicine woman, but she barely gets any into him.

Late in the evening, the fever intensifies. That night, my brother-in-law exchanges the temporary for the eternal.

Kate, the twins, and I are sitting in the tent around the fire in the morning.

"What will happen now?" Kate wonders aloud.

The children cling sadly to Kate's skirts. They don't want to go to school but also don't know what to do here. Occasionally, they look shyly at the bed where their father lies motionless, covered with a sheet.

Paul has gone to Duncan to call our parents and arrange for the undertaker to come.

"Do you think he suffered when he died?" Kate asks. "Do you think he felt lonely?"

"I don't know," I say honestly. "He wasn't restless late at night. Maybe he just slipped away quietly," I try to comfort her.

Kate dries the tears that have slowly fallen from her cheeks onto her hands. She blows her nose and stands up. "Is it strange if we go have some coffee? We need to do something, right?"

"I think it's fine," I say. "Our lives go on, you know. We need to start eating and drinking again."

"Exactly," Kate says. "It doesn't help to sit around moping." She takes the kettle with water and hangs it over the fire. I also get up and start tidying up. The twins begin some mending work. We try to avoid looking at Dylan's dead body, which is so prominently and yet so quietly present.

Sooner than expected, we hear a horse and wagon coming up the road. It stops on the path. A man dressed in black enters the tent behind Paul. He condoles with us with extreme politeness, to the point of being painful. I understand that he is trying to gauge the situation and, especially, the degree of grief. Some people are relieved; others feel as if they can't go on living. I'm not sure which group Kate belongs to. I personally feel little sorrow over the loss of my brother-in-law; rather, I feel sorrow for Kate, who now has to manage everything alone with the little ones. Paul keeps to the side. He, too, is assessing the situation.

Kate answers the questions the undertaker asks her.

Meanwhile, Paul tells me about his phone call with Dad. "Your father is going to Dylan's parents to inform them of his death. Tomorrow, your father and Dylan's parents will take the ferry and come here. Your mother is unable to make the trip. The day after tomorrow, the funeral will take place."

I reflect on how good it is that Paul has traveled with us and is supporting us in this bizarre situation. I briefly hold his hand.

❧

The following day, Dad and Dylan's parents arrive and check into the elegant Mount Sicker Hotel.

The next day, the undertaker's wagon, carrying the casket, slowly descends the mountain. Kate and I walk directly behind it. The twins each have a child in tow. Following them are Dylan's parents, Dad, and Paul. Olga and Amber are also present. At the very back are Fred and Teacher Jelle. We move slowly down the hill. It seems never-ending. Halfway down, the snow has melted, except for a few patches.

At the foot of the hill, we board a wagon that the undertaker has parked there. We follow the casket to Mount View Cemetery, the Methodist graveyard in Duncan.

On the plot reserved for graves are a few stones and some white wooden crosses scattered around. We form a circle around the open grave that will be Dylan's final resting place. A thin layer of water sits at the bottom of the grave. Like our feelings, the sky is grey and dreary. Daisy and Bobby cling to Rose and Jasmin's arms.

Teacher Jelle, acting as the minister for this occasion, reads from John 11: "I am the Resurrection and the Life; he who believes in Me, though he may die, he shall live."

I sigh silently. My thoughts tumble over each other, and I no longer hear what Teacher Jelle continues to say. Did Dylan

156

believe in the Lord Jesus? He came from a Christian background, but does that guarantee that he believed Jesus had died and risen for him? Isn't there a Bible verse that says you'll know a tree by its fruit? Honestly, nothing comes to mind that indicates Dylan bore good fruit, except perhaps that he fulfilled his duty to provide for his family. Even that is questionable now that I've heard about his debts. Where is he now? Suddenly, sweat breaks out on my forehead, and I force myself not to think further in that direction.

Fred stands broodingly, watching Kate. What thoughts are running through his mind? Fred is also scrutinizing Olga from head to toe. I see that she looks away from him and nervously fiddles with her scarf.

The children sob. Apart from their sniffling and Teacher Jelle's calm voice, the flat field is silent. Even the birds keep their beaks closed as if they understand the gravity of the situation. Kate's face looks pale beneath her black hat, but she doesn't shed a tear. Suddenly, I think of the mother of a child in my class. She had been a widow for a few months.

"Grieving comes later," she said. "Only after you've dealt with all the formalities can you think about how it was, grieve over how it might have been, feel your fear and worry for the uncertain, anxious future. Only when everything and everyone around you returns to the old normal, and you're left alone with your grief, does it really start to gnaw at you. When you notice your children desperately trying to get back to normal life while you, unlike them, don't want to go on. You need rest, but then people knock on the door of your attention. It distracts you from your grief, but sometimes your grief grows because you have to do it all yourself and alone. Suddenly, it falls like a stone on your head and heart, and you gasp for breath as you try to master the anxiety of what comes next."

Poor Kate. I put an arm around her shoulders and pull her close. We silently watch as the pallbearers lower the casket into the grave. The undertaker throws the first shovelful of dirt onto the casket. With a dull thud, the earth hits the wood of the lid. It pounds in my ears.

"Let's go," says Kate.

Daisy, Bobby, and Amber each pick a flower from a hellebore growing beside one of the graves and toss them onto the casket. Then they walk with us back to the road where the wagon is waiting. We walk slowly and occasionally stop to read a tombstone: "Rest in Peace," "Forever in Our Thoughts," "Safe in the Arms of Jesus," "Until We Meet Again," "Sleeping with the Angels," "Forever Loved."

What would Kate want on Dylan's gravestone? "Gone but Not Forgotten"? "In God's Care"?

Perhaps she will never replace the white wooden cross with just Dylan's name, birth, and death dates, which the undertaker had already placed at the grave. Maybe she will never have enough money to buy a proper stone.

The wagon takes us back up the mountain. The horse stops in the middle of the village. Olga and Amber get out.

"All the best," Olga says to Kate. "If I can help with anything, just let me know."

"Thank you for coming to the funeral," Kate says. "I really appreciate it."

Kate also thanks Fred when he gets out at the tents a little later.

"I want to talk to you," Fred says to Kate.

Kate looks at him, surprised and questioning. Fred says nothing and waits until Dad, Dylan's parents, Paul, I, and the children have exited and gone into the tent. Through a gap in the tent fabric, I see his animated gestures. I am curious about what he has to say, but I'll have to wait until I'm alone with Kate. That moment comes only after the neighbour women have visited to offer their condolences. They brought enough food for the entire week and stayed for lunch.

Once everyone has gone home, Dad and Dylan's parents have returned to the hotel, and the children are playing outside, I approach Kate directly to ask what Fred had to say this morning.

Kate is fiddling with the dishes the neighbours brought and arranging them on the table next to the fire.

"He asked..." she finally says after a confusing silence. "He wants to take over my piece of land."

For a moment, I'm unsure what to think. "Is this good or bad?" I ask myself.

Kate mentions the amount Fred offered her. "It's only a quarter of what Dylan paid for it. How could it have depreciated so much in a few months?" she ponders aloud.

"Fred told me that if I sold the land for that price, I would be completely free of debt to him. He told me about the money Dylan lost gambling and that he had borrowed from Fred."

She falls silent and shifts a few more dishes.

I walk over to her and take her hands in mine. "Forget about the dishes for now," I say gently. "Have you decided what you want to do?"

"I'll look up the purchase contract from the mining company. I need to think about it. I don't know yet," Kate sighs.

"How much did Dylan actually owe Fred?" I ask.

"I don't know," Kate says, embarrassed. "I didn't ask Dylan about it, and he obviously didn't tell me. I wasn't assertive enough," she says sadly. "I should have kept a closer eye on him. I should have kept him away from Fred and the pub." Her voice begins to tremble. I put my arm around her and hold her close.

We remain like this until Paul comes in, having taken Dad and Dylan's parents back to the hotel. "Sorry," he says. "I didn't mean to interrupt you."

"No, no," says Kate, drying her eyes with a corner of her apron, "you're not disturbing us. Maybe you can even help us."

"Okay," Paul says, sounding curious. Then, to lighten the mood, he adds, "How can I be of service?"

Kate explains Fred's offer to buy her land. "That way, I would be free of Dylan's gambling debt."

Paul asks the same questions I did.

Kate shrugs sadly. "I'll look up the contract and ask Fred how much the debt is."

It begins to grow dark. I put the food the neighbours brought into the Dutch oven and hang it over the fire.

The funeral is a few days behind us, and we're trying to pick up the threads of everyday life again.

This morning, I drop Daisy and Bobby off at school. Teacher Jelle walks through the schoolyard. Amber greets Daisy at the gate. Together, they run up to their teacher.

"We'd like to know what the stones look like that the men are searching for in the mines," I hear them say.

"Ah, yes," says the teacher, thoughtfully placing a fingertip on his lips while his other hand supports his elbow.

"You know," he says, "would you like to come with me to the mining company office this afternoon?"

The girls look at each other in surprise and jump up with excitement. "Yes, that sounds great! We'd love to."

"Alright then," says the teacher, "I'll see you this afternoon after school."

The girls happily run back into the schoolyard.

"Are you coming along too?" the teacher asks me.

I nod. "That seems very interesting. It's good for the girls to have a distraction from the sadness of the past few days."

After school, the girls skip to the mining office, while the teacher and I walk behind them. Shyly and curiously, they step through the door the teacher holds open for us. Behind a wooden table sits a man who greets us warmly. "So, teacher, ladies, what can I do for you?"

"Hello, Dave," says the teacher. "These girls would like to know what the rocks look like that the men are mining for."

"Well, I can show you that," says Dave. "Come on."

He steps out from behind his desk and gestures for them to follow him to a corner of the office. There, in a display case, lie rough stones. One by one, he takes the stones out of the case.

"This is gold, and this is silver," he says, holding the stones out to the girls.

The girls examine the stones closely. They're allowed to hold them, turning them around in their hands and inspecting them from all angles.

"How do you tell what's what?" Amber asks. "They all look so similar."

"That's true," says Dave. "But if you look closely, you can see the colour of gold or silver in the stone. And copper is much redder, see?"

"I see it now," says Amber.

"How deep underground is the ore?" Daisy asks.

"Sometimes very deep, sometimes right on the surface," Dave explains. "When the first gold prospectors—Sullivan, MacKay, and Buzzard—came from America, they dug for a long time and didn't find much. They named the pieces of land they bought Alice, Lenora, Belle, and Gold Queen. In the summer of August 1896, a huge forest fire destroyed their huts and most of their tools. They had to run for their lives. Discouraged, they left their land, and it seemed like everything would go back to the way it was before. A friend of theirs, who lived in the area, came later back to the mountain. He saw that the fire had exposed a large piece of copper, right on the surface. He also found traces of gold and silver. That's how things started here, just a few years ago." The girls listen attentively.

"Now," says the teacher, "do the lady researchers have any more questions?"

The girls shake their heads.

"Thank you for showing us the precious stones," Daisy says politely.

"Thank you for everything you've just told us," adds Amber.

"No thanks needed. Feel free to come by again if you have more questions."

"Thank you, Dave," says the teacher. "Perhaps you could come to the class and talk about the mining company."

"I'll think about it," promises Dave.

We all walk outside again.

"Enjoy your dinner, ladies, and see you tomorrow," the teacher says.

"Goodbye, teacher, see you tomorrow!" the girls call out.

"Enjoy your dinner too, and thank you!" they add.

"Goodbye, Elsa, see you tomorrow." Teacher Jelle tips his hat and walks away, smiling.

162

I follow the girls as they dance ahead of me. Beautiful golden rays of sunshine peek over the mountain's edge in the distance before the sun sets for the night.

෧෴ඏ

"Now we know where to look," Daisy says to Amber as we walk home. "We have an hour to dig before the sun completely goes down."

Arriving at the tent, the girls run to the spot behind the tent where Fred and Dylan were digging when Dylan was still alive. Rose follows them curiously.

Kate isn't home yet. She works at the Brenton Hotel until the mine whistle blows. Bobby is playing at a friend's house.

I linger for a moment to watch the girls.

"Give me a shovel, too," says Rose. "I'll help with the digging."

The girls dance around. Rose is much stronger than they are. The girls each grab one of the shovels lying on the ground and hand one to Rose.

"We need to start somewhere here because Fred and my father were digging in this spot," Daisy says, pointing to a large hole in the ground.

Down in the valley, the lamps are being lit. Above the mountain, the rosy glow of the setting sun is still visible.

"Hurry, dig before the sun is gone," Daisy tells Amber.

They pick up the heavy shovels again and thrust them into the ground. With their feet, they push the shovels farther. The ground is rock-hard, and they have to jump on the shovels with both feet to push them a few centimeters farther into the earth. Rose has picked up a pickaxe and is hacking away at the ground with great enthusiasm. The girls stop occasionally to wipe their hair, which has come loose from their braids, out of their faces.

"Phew," says Amber. "I'm getting warm from this."

Daisy pokes around in the hole. She sees something glittering. "Look," she says, "what's that?"

The girls bend down into the shallow hole and reach for the loose pieces of ground that sparkle in the twilight.

"I'll take a piece to school," Daisy says.

"Good idea," Amber agrees. "Then we can ask the teacher what it is."

Daisy puts the stone in the pocket of her coat. I've been watching the girls for a while and go inside to help Jasmin prepare dinner. Rose disappears into the outhouse.

I've just gotten inside when I hear a harsh voice outside. I cautiously peek around the tent door.

"So, what are you girls doing here?" Fred asks as he walks up.

The girls look at him with alarm. "Nothing," Daisy stammers. "We're just playing here."

"Hmmm, I think it's time for you to go inside; it's getting dark," Fred grumbles.

The girls jump up, dust the dirt off their hands, and start to leave. Then Amber, suddenly brave but also a bit defiant, asks, "What are you doing here anyway?"

For a moment, Fred seems taken aback. I see a fierce fire in his eyes.

I hold my breath and stand ready to intervene if he makes a wrong move.

"Aren't you that little girl from Olga at the hotel?" he asks slowly and threateningly. "You care about your mother, don't you?"

Amber nods.

"Then make sure you don't lose her."

Confused, Amber looks at Daisy. Daisy looks equally bewildered. Amber nods almost imperceptibly.

"Then I'd be careful if I were you," Fred threatens again.

The girls start running. Panting, they roll into the tent and collapse on the mat just behind the tent door. They slam the tent flap shut. Then they start nervously laughing but soon become angry.

"What does that guy think he's doing?" Amber fumes.

Then Rose enters the tent. "I heard what that crazy man said to you. What kind of threat was that? What does your mother have to do with it?" she asks indignantly.

"Girls, listen," I say. "I also heard what he said to you. Fred is a dangerous man. You need to promise me you'll stay away from him. And all of us, including you, Rose," I add firmly.

I wait for an answer, and somewhat reluctantly, the girls agree. They promise to avoid Fred.

Rose is furious. "I'm going to confront him and tell him the truth."

"No," I say, grabbing her until she calms down a bit.

"He shouldn't think he can get away with this," she continues to mutter angrily.

The girls have become afraid of Fred and what he might do to Amber's mother. I'm worried, too. The women at the hotel are already in an uncertain and especially unsafe position.

Kate and I walk the children to school the next morning. It's Friday, and Kate has the day off. We plan to stop by the Brenton Hotel later to ask Olga to come to our tent that evening.

"I'll ask Teacher Jelle if he wants to come too," I say. "He needs to know that Fred has threatened Amber."

Before we drop the kids off in the schoolyard, we stop by the Mount Sicker Hotel, where Dad and Dylan's parents are staying. They are heading back to Vancouver today, and the children say their goodbyes.

"Goodbye, Daisy, goodbye, Bobby," says Dad, giving the children a hug. "Will you be careful?"

The children nod. Dylan's parents also hug the kids. Dylan's mother has red eyes and a blotchy face from crying. Dylan's father struggles to control his emotions.

"Mom," Kate says to her mother-in-law, "we'll come back later to say goodbye before you head to Duncan with the grocer."

"That's fine," she says, holding Kate's hands tightly. "Please come back to Vancouver as soon as you can," she adds urgently. "This is no place for young women and children."

Kate nods. "I have a few things to take care of, and then I'll make plans to come back."

"Good," the fathers agree in unison. "If you need help, don't forget that you can ask us." "It's nice that they don't blame you for coming here," I say to Kate as we continue toward the school. "They'll welcome you with open arms in Vancouver."

That evening, as we all sit around the fire, we tell Olga, Paul, and Teacher Jelle about what happened the previous night. "You need to be careful," warns the teacher.

We all agree. Kate seems lost in thought but nods in agreement.

"I don't trust that guy at all," says Olga when I finish my story. "Let me tell you what happened at the hotel."

One evening, shortly after the mining disaster, when Dylan was still alive, Fred was at the hotel. He was drinking at the bar. The women usually leave him alone. They avoid that hothead.

That evening, I had a mission. I'd heard the rumors about the mining disaster. Since Amber had become friends with Daisy, I wanted to find out what was true. "Hi, Fred," I said flirtatiously as I took a seat on the barstool next to him.

Fred didn't pay much attention to me until I mentioned that a room upstairs was available and asked if he wanted to come along. Fred looked up, somewhat surprised. He usually has to beg the girls. In one gulp, he emptied his glass and slammed it on the bar. He stood up and puffed out his chest, clearly feeling the man.

For a moment, I was taken aback and wondered: What have you gotten yourself into, girl?

He followed me up the stairs to the pampering rooms like a proud rooster. While I gave him attention and tried to put him at ease, I casually asked him a few questions.

"It must have been a terrible experience in the mine," I said, "especially to see your friend in so much pain and not be able to do anything to ease it."

To buy time, I poured a drink from a decanter on a small table by the bed. I poured myself a glass, too. I refilled Fred's glass before I'd even taken more than a small sip of mine. Fred downed his glass in one gulp.

"It wasn't that bad," he said abruptly.

"No?" I asked cautiously. "I thought you were good friends."

"Oh, we are, but he has so much that I don't."

I paused before asking more questions, trying not to sound too curious. I looked at him over the rim of my glass. "What does he have that you don't?" I asked.

"Well," Fred said, suddenly surly, "a beautiful wife, a good piece of land, an inheritance. I don't have any of that. Everyone is always against me. My parents didn't know what they were doing when they raised me, and I always got into trouble at school."

"You don't want to see your friend suffer, even if he has more than you, do you?" I ventured.

"It's not fair," Fred slurred.

"Not fair?" I asked, throwing some more oil on the fire. "Life is unfair, isn't it?"

"As unfair as you allow it to be," Fred growled. "From now on, I'm taking justice into my own hands because no one does anything about all the wrongs done to me," he said defiantly.

"How are you going to do that?" I asked, stroking his broad chest.

"Huh," he said, sitting up straighter. "I'm not telling you that, but what I will tell you,"—he waved his finger in front of my face, making me pull back a bit—"is that what I've started has a purpose. And," he said mysteriously, "I've found an important person who will help me achieve my goal."

I hesitated, unsure whether to ask the next question that lingered in my mind.

But I asked anyway. "Did you take justice into your own hands when you were in the mine?"

Again, Fred waved his finger in front of my nose. "You don't interfere with my business, understand?" he said, his voice low and threatening.

Then, just as suddenly, his mood shifted, and he said as sweetly as he could, "Come on, we're not here to talk about business."

Without warning, he grabbed me and pushed me onto the bed. I didn't struggle. In the back of my mind, I heard my boss's voice: "Don't resist guys like Fred, or you'll be dead in no time."

None of us knows what to say when Olga finishes her story. A nauseous knot twists in my stomach. Kate looks pale, almost ghostly white.

"The girls must absolutely stay away from that man," Olga emphasizes. "He's life-threatening dangerous."

Kate pours tea. "Would you mind taking a look at our land behind the tent tomorrow?" she asks Paul. "The girls dug and found some stones. You know about rocks and might be able to tell if they've found something special."

"Let me see," Paul says, turning to the girls.

Daisy pulls out the stone she found behind the tent and shows it to Paul.

Paul takes the stone, turns it around, and scrapes a bit of dirt off with his nail. Then he stares at Daisy and Amber for a few seconds.

"What?" they ask. "What is it?"

I also watch him with interest, curious if it might be a valuable mineral.

"This," Paul says slowly, "this is silver ore."

For a moment, we are speechless.

"Wow," Daisy and Amber say at the same time.

My head starts spinning. "Kate, you shouldn't sell your land to Fred for the price he's asking. He probably knows there's something valuable on it," I say anxiously.

"It has become a lot more dangerous for us now. Do you realize that?" Paul asks.

We stare at him.

"Why?" Daisy asks.

"Because," Paul says, "the land is probably worth a lot, and if Fred finds out what you've discovered, he'll do anything to get his hands on it. The land might be worth much more than the debts your father owed him."

Paul pauses for a moment.

"We mustn't tell anyone anything," he continues. "If anyone lets something slip to Fred, we'll be in big trouble." He looks intently at the girls. "Can you promise not to say anything to your friends or anyone else?"

The girls nod.

I see concern in their eyes.

It's gotten late, and Teacher Jelle takes Olga and Amber to the hotel before heading home to his landlady. Kate sits down and takes the Bible from the table next to her.

"What are you reading?" I ask as she opens the Bible.

"Here in Matthew," she replies, "it says we shouldn't worry. It's good to be reminded of that, especially now that I have so many questions and fears and don't know what decisions to make."

With a sigh, she later puts the Bible back on the table. I suddenly have a strange premonition, as if something unusual is about to happen and our lives are about to take a different turn.

"And," I ask Paul the next Monday, "was there any news in the village today?"

"Oh yes," he says teasingly, "but I can't tell you. You'll have to read it in the newspaper."

"What?" I exclaim. "The newspaper? It gets here days later, by which time it's already outdated."

"You're right," Paul chuckles. "I'll give you a little hint every time something exciting happens. The rest you'll have to read for yourself."

"I'm very grateful to you," I say mockingly, but I can't help but laugh at him.

Before the children go to bed, Jasmin cuts a slice of the pumpkin bread that she and Rose baked today for everyone.

"Is this the recipe Aunt Margaret gave you?" I ask the twins.

"Yes," Jasmin replies. "I only had to adjust a few ingredients because they weren't in stock at the store."

"It tastes delicious after a day of hard work," I say approvingly.

Then, it's time for the children to go to sleep. Jasmin tucks them in and reads them a story from the Bible.

Once the children are settled, Paul talks about the visits he made to the mining office, the shops, and the pub in the village, having managed to gather information everywhere.

"I'm going to write another article for the newspaper tonight," he says, "and I have enough for an extra one."

"Can I read it before you send it off tomorrow? Or is it still a secret, and should I wait for it to appear in the newspaper in a few days?" I ask teasingly.

"You can read it, but you have to promise not to tell anyone. The newspaper doesn't want to publish old news."

"I promise," I say.

Paul grabs his notepad and pen and starts on his article. Daisy wakes up and can't fall back asleep. She leans over Paul's shoulder and reads along. Paul lets her. It feels very homely. Kate has gone to the far corner of the tent to lie on her bed. The fire pit is between her and us, so she's not disturbed by us. It's quiet in Bobby's bed. Jasmin writes in her diary, and Rose is trying to carve something from wood.

"Ouch," Rose says suddenly, putting her finger in her mouth.

Jasmin looks up, alarmed. "Did you hurt yourself?" she asks worriedly.

"It's fine," Rose says, waving her hand. Then she picks up the piece of wood and the knife again and starts carving more.

By the glow of the fire, Paul writes his last lines. He hands the paper to me. My eyes slowly scan the lines. Paul moves the lantern, which is almost out and flickering suspiciously, closer to me. It doesn't help much.

"Look," I say, "maybe you should adjust this line a bit."

Paul leans over the text as he sits next to me on the bed. We read through it together, line by line. Paul makes some changes based on my suggestions and leaves others unchanged. After we finish, he stands up to return to his own tent.

"Thank you," he whispers. "I enjoyed working together."

"I did, too," I whisper back. "Good night, I'll see you tomorrow."

Paul gathers his writing materials, opens the tent door, and heads back to his own tent. I tuck Daisy into bed and soon fall into a deep sleep with a satisfied feeling.

౭౿౿

The next morning, I wake up to Kate throwing a new log on the smoldering fire. The tent feels damp from the six people breathing their moist breath into the air all night and from the laundry drying next to the stove. Kate opens the tent door a bit and looks outside into the still half-dark morning sky.

"Look," she says, gesturing for me to come over.

I crawl out of bed and groan as I lift my aching body. I peek through the crack in the tent door and see a doe with her two fawns standing there. They've heard us and are now standing stiff as statues, staring at our tent. Only their ears move back and forth. Then they decide they've been worried for nothing and continue their search for food, sniffing through the snow. Suddenly, as if an invisible bomb has exploded, all three of them flee. They dance through the snow, taking hilarious leaps with their white tails held high, before disappearing down the mountain slope.

Bobby has also woken up and turns over once more. Daisy is still asleep.

The morning routine repeats itself. The twins stay home to take care of the laundry and prepare the food. Kate and I take the children to school together, and then Kate goes off to work.

Before Kate disappears through the back door of the hotel, I suddenly say, "I'm so glad you're my sister, that we're family."

A smile spreads across Kate's face as she places her basket on the ground and opens her arms wide for a big hug.

"We will always be friends and sisters, right?" she asks, close to my ear.

"Yes, forever," I say.

I feel grateful to have a sister who loves me.

We've had a day of hard work. Kate and I sit with the twins by the fire in the tent. The laundry is drying on the rack next to the fire pit. It's damp and smoky inside. The events of the past few days weigh on our minds.

A harsh cough is heard from the corner where Daisy is lying in bed. Kate looks up with concern. When Daisy coughs again, Kate gets up to check on her. Daisy turns over and continues to sleep.

Kate returns to her chair by the fire.

"If she's still coughing like this tomorrow, we should visit the medicine woman," I say. "The rosemary and thyme tea I gave her isn't working quickly enough."

"Do you think she'll see us?" Kate asks worriedly.

"Don't forget it wasn't your fault Dylan refused to use her medicine. You did everything you could to help him. He was too stubborn to accept it," I say, somewhat irritated.

"Daisy is sick now and needs help. Please don't feel guilty about a decision that wasn't yours. He paid with his life, and as harsh as it sounds, it was his own fault," Rose says.

A tense silence settles over the tent.

"Sorry," Rose says, her voice softer, "that did sound rather heartless."

"You're right," Kate says sadly.

Her face still carries some doubt, but suddenly, concern for Daisy prevails, and she says decisively, "We're going to the medicine woman tomorrow. I can't risk losing my girl."

That night, I hear Kate getting out of bed several times to give Daisy something to drink.

In the morning, Daisy doesn't have the energy to get out of bed, so the twins take Bobby to school.

"Shall I go to the medicine woman so you can stay with Daisy?" I ask Kate.

"No, I'll come with you," she replies. "I want to thank her personally. I feel guilty that Dylan treated her so poorly. Daisy will be fine here with the twins. Rose and Jasmin will be back soon."

Kate places a cup of warm tea with honey beside Daisy. "Don't get out of bed until we're back," she commands.

"Okay, Mom," Daisy says softly. Her little face is flushed with fever.

Kate wraps a piece of cheese, potatoes, carrots, beets, and onions in a large, beautiful white damask tea towel she brought from Vancouver to take to the medicine woman as a gift.

Rose and Jasmin return to the tent, and Kate tucks Daisy in once more. After giving a few more instructions to the twins, she closes the tent door, and we walk along the muddy, puddle-filled path down to the road that leads to the foot of the mountain. It's a clear morning, and from the top of the mountain, we have a good view of the valley. To our left is the water of the bay, with the mountains of Salt Spring Island behind it, and to the south, the mainland of America. In the valley, around Somenos Lake, up to Maple Bay, we see plumes of smoke rising into the air. These are from the pioneer farms that dot the valley. The few plumes of smoke farther south are from the fires at the First Nations tipis.

Paul told me that not long ago, the First Nations village stretched over a distance of twenty kilometers between Somenos Lake and Cowichan Bay, and then farther inland to Lake Cowichan. Due to a smallpox outbreak brought to the valley by the pioneers, only a hundred of the once fifteen thousand First Nations people remained.

In the middle of the First Nations territory, we see Duncan, the town that has exploded in growth with the arrival of the mining town on Mount Sicker.

We continue down the mountain. Wagonloads of ore pass us on their way to the gondolas leading to the trains. The men on the wagons greet us by lifting their cowboy hats. Their dark faces observe us with interest.

After about an hour, we arrive at the foot of the mountain. We find the narrow path through the undergrowth leading to a group of tipis. Above the vegetation, we see the smoke from a wood fire burning by the tents. I inhale the scents of burning pine wood and smoked salmon, which become stronger as we get closer.

Suddenly, we find ourselves at the edge of a clearing with three wigwams. In the center of the clearing, a pot hangs over a fire. Next to the fire, a First Nations man is sitting on the ground. He holds a stick of beautiful arbutus wood in one hand. With the knife in his other hand, he carves figures into the wood. He sings softly to himself while swaying slowly back and forth. It sounds like "Hujehujehuje." When he sees us, he spits into the fire. On the other side of the fire, a young woman is knitting. I smile at her in an attempt to break the ice. She stands up, revealing a piece of grey clothing with the pattern of a black cougar. With a nod of her head, she directs the children, who have been peeking at us with their black eyes and dirty brown faces from behind her, to the tent. They get up and sprint inside. The man also stands and goes into the tent.

We cautiously step forward. "We've come to bring a gift to thank the medicine woman for the medicine she gave us when my husband was ill," Kate says.

The woman turns and walks to one of the other tipis. She sticks her head into the tent opening and says something in

Hul'q'umi'num, the language of the Coast Salish people. Without looking at us again, she disappears into the tent where the man and children went. The clearing is now empty.

We stand there awkwardly, waiting. Occasionally, I see a little head with messy black hair appear at the entrance of the family tent. I hear the father calling the child back. I'm surprised that these people still speak their own language. I know the government has long been working hard to integrate the First Nations into the English system. One of the goals is to make the Hul'q'umi'num language disappear. Deep in my heart, I'm glad these people are resisting the government's goal.

While I ponder this, the medicine woman emerges from the other tipi and approaches us. She is a short, stout woman leaning on a beautiful walking stick carved from the wood of an arbutus tree. A colourful cloth is tied around her head, and a thick, knitted cape with traditional Coast Salish figures is draped over her shoulders. She doesn't acknowledge us but walks directly to the fire and begins to stir the pot hanging over it. Kate and I, somewhat familiar with First Nations customs, wait quietly until the old woman initiates the conversation. As she stirs, she sings just like the man: "Hujehujehuje, Hujehujehuje."

Then she stands up and looks at us. Kate steps forward and offers her the gift. The medicine woman ignores it. Kate explains again that she has come to thank the medicine woman for the medicine and to apologize for Dylan's behaviour.

The medicine woman nods. "He better?" she asks.

"No," Kate replies sadly. "He's gone."

"Back to Creator," the old woman says, pointing upwards.

Our eyes follow her finger. High in the sky, an eagle soars on the wind.

"Now my little girl is sick," Kate says. "I wanted to ask if you have medicine for her."

"Sick?" asks the old woman.

"She has a bad cough and fever," Kate replies.

The woman nods and resumes stirring the pot as she sings.

"Cough, fever, snot?" she asks again.

Kate nods.

The woman turns and walks to the edge of the clearing, where a white pine tree stands. Her singing grows louder as she approaches the tree. Carefully, she picks some needles between her thumb and forefinger and yanks them off the branch. She collects a few more bunches of needles from different parts of the tree. She also scrapes some resin from the trunk. Returning to the fire, she picks up a piece of arbutus bark from the ground. Slowly, she walks toward us, taking Kate's hand as she stands before us. Kate quickly hands me the tea towel with the gift.

The old woman places the needles, resin, and bark in Kate's open hand. Then, she folds it closed and, with both hands, cradles Kate's hand as if to say, "Don't lose them. They are sacred."

"Boil water," the old woman says. "Pour it over the needles, resin, and bark. Let it steep, and drink it every day. You too," she commands, pointing her finger from me to Kate and back.

We nod and thank her. I hand her the tea towel with the gift, which she accepts this time.

"Thank you," we say again as we slowly step backward.

From the opening of the tent, I see curious black eyes peering out, and I smile at them. They disappear immediately. I hear a soft giggle followed by a reprimand from their father.

The old woman is still in the same spot as we begin our way back, and I glance once more at the edge of the clearing. I cautiously nod to her as a greeting, but there is no response. Uncomfortably, we begin the climb out of the valley that leads to the road going up the mountain. It isn't until we are halfway up the mountain that I can shake off the impression that the medicine woman is no longer following us with her eyes.

Kate and I haven't spoken yet, so impressed are we by what we have just experienced.

"Pine needles?" Kate says suddenly, incredulous. "Pine needles are supposed to make Daisy better?"

I shrug. "Let's just give it a try," I say. "I know the bark of the arbutus is good for a sore throat, so the rest must be good for something too."

We continue climbing up the mountain. Empty wagons, having dropped off their loads of ore and wood at the train below, rumble past us. I turn my face away from the dust that blows up from the road.

Then I see something moving on the steep slope beside the road. Is it a deer? I dismiss that thought. It's far too busy on the road right now. Deer only come when the noise of the wagons is gone after working hours.

I take another look. Is that a person sitting in the bushes? Then it moves, and I see it's a First Nations boy. He wobbles and takes a few steps, then sinks back to the ground.

"Look, Kate," I point out. "That boy must not be feeling well. I'm going to see if he needs help."

We scramble down the slope until we reach the boy, who is now sitting on the ground.

He looks pale. He gazes at us fearfully and gestures defensively with his hands. "No, no," he says.

"What's wrong?" I ask. "Do you feel sick?"

179

"I want to go home. I want to go home," he says urgently.

He tries to stand again but fails.

"Where is your home?" I ask.

He points south. "At the foot of the mountain," he says weakly.

"Kate," I say, "you go to Daisy with the medicine. I'll help this boy to his home."

We support the boy and head toward the road.

"No, no," the boy says again, "don't walk on the road."

Suddenly, a light goes on in my head, and I ask, "Where did you come from?"

The boy shakes his head. Apparently, he doesn't want to tell.

"You go on," I say to Kate. "We'll manage."

I want to be alone with the boy to ask him more questions. Kate climbs farther up to the road. At the top, she looks down once more, and I nod at her. "I'll be back as soon as I can," I call out.

Then Kate disappears into a dust cloud from a wagon rumbling by.

I take the boy by the arm, and together we slowly make our way through the vegetation on the steep slope. Whenever we hear a wagon coming, we crouch on the ground and wait for it to pass. Slowly, very slowly, we make progress. We reach the foot of the mountain. Now we need to cross the road. I strain my ears to listen for any approaching vehicles. Although I still don't know why the boy doesn't want to be seen, I have a strong suspicion. We cross the road as quickly as we can and disappear into the vegetation where the narrow path to the First Nations camp begins. As soon as we can no longer see the road, the boy lets out a sigh of relief.

"Why are you so scared?" I dare to ask.

The boy shakes his head again. He stumbles along on my arm, and just before the clearing, he says, "Go away, go away."

Then my teacher's stubbornness kicks in, and with a stern voice, I say, "No, I'm taking you all the way home."

The woman knitting and the man working with wood sit again by the fire. The children are running around. Suddenly, one of the children starts calling out. The man and woman both look up and see us approaching. They stand up and run to the boy. The woman embraces him while I watch from a distance.

Then the man comes threateningly toward me, growling something in the Hul'q'umi'num language. I don't understand him and take a startled step back. The commotion has also drawn the old woman outside. She approaches me and the threatening man. Gesturing vigorously and speaking intensely, he explains the situation to her. The old woman calms him down. Angrily, he turns away and goes to the boy.

The old woman begins to speak. "Don't tell anyone he's here," she says.

I shake my head. Then I ask her the question I wanted to ask the boy. "Did he run away from school?"

The old woman looks at me intensely. Her gaze intimidates me.

"Don't tell anyone," she says again, confirming my suspicion.

"I won't tell anyone," I promise, placing my hand on my heart.

I walk back to the path. Once more, I look back and see the children dancing. The man follows me with dark eyes. I nod at the old woman.

"Don't tell anyone," she says once more.

At the road, I look extra carefully to see if anyone is coming. Then I hurry across the road and up the mountain.

Thoughts swirl in my head. Did I do the right thing by helping the boy? Isn't it important that Indigenous people also receive a good education and learn how to deal with the new English civilization? Doubts start to creep in, questioning why First Nations children have to be sent so far from home to school. Why can't they attend school in Duncan or on the mountain? Why aren't they allowed to speak their own language? Why must their First Nations names be changed to English?

By the time I reach Kate's tent, it's lunchtime. My rumbling stomach makes me irritable and outraged at the government, which has been trying for so many years to change and even destroy Indigenous culture.

I see Kate standing in front of the tent. Mr. Jelle is with her. He must be asking about Daisy's condition.

"Hello," I greet them both as I come within hearing distance.

"Were you able to get the boy home?" Kate asks.

I nod and try to enter the tent. I don't want to talk. I promised the medicine woman not to speak about her grandson.

Apparently, Kate has told Mr. Jelle about the incident because he asks, "Shouldn't that boy be in school? What was he doing in the bushes?"

"He's sick," is all I want to say.

I try to enter the tent again.

"Elsa," Mr. Jelle says in a stern tone.

Surprised by his lecturing tone, I look at him.

"First Nations children must go to school too, just like English children. You shouldn't help them skip school," he says.

Deep inside, I feel my anger growing. Elsa, I tell myself, try to hold back. Don't say things you'll regret later.

"Well," I say sarcastically, "could the teacher explain to me why First Nations children are sent all the way to Port Alberni or even farther away from their parents to go to school? Huh?" I ask challengingly when he doesn't answer right away.

"The government has decided that it's best for the First Nations to be in school together," he responds weakly.

"The government, huh?" I say angrily. "Since when does the English government know what's best for people of a different culture? Have they forgotten that the First Nations were here first and that they just took over their land? That they are in the process of destroying their culture?"

"You're going too far," Mr. Jelle says. "It's for their own good that they receive a good education."[1]

---

[1] The thoughts Elsa expresses here are based on the contemporary belief that all Indigenous children experienced abuse during their time at residential schools. In-depth research has shown that the opinion held by Mr. Jelle is closer to the truth. Most Indigenous children attended day schools, allowing them to be with their families on weekends and during holidays. The majority of the classes consisted of a mixed group of Indigenous and white children. Generally, the children were encouraged to speak English but were not punished for speaking their own language. There is no evidence that more Indigenous children died at residential schools compared to those attending public schools. If more children did die at residential schools, it was partly because sick children were placed in hospitals associated with the schools instead of traveling home. Overall, the teachers at these schools provided knowledge and skills that the children otherwise would not have received. (Information sourced from True North Canada News.)

"You're nuts," I say and disappear into the tent. I don't want to talk about this topic anymore.

"Why are you angry?" a small voice comes from the bed in the corner.

I go to the sick child. "Don't worry. That was an adult problem. Do you want something to drink?"

I take the mug with tea, and Daisy takes a sip. Throughout the day, we give her the medicine prescribed by the medicine woman.

The next morning, Daisy is sitting up in bed. She's still too weak to go to school, but at least she's improving. We've all taken the medicine, and so far, no one else has become ill.

Kate sits on the bed next to Daisy and gives her a hug. "I'm so glad you're feeling better," she says, tears in her eyes.

I walk with Bobby to school and then head to the grocery store for some errands. In the schoolyard, Mr. Jelle is walking around. I give him a curt nod of greeting. The expression on his face betrays no hint of his thoughts. After I've done the shopping, I head back and walk past the school to Kate's tent. The children and the teacher have gone inside; classes have started. I hear a horse approaching behind me. I step aside to let the rider pass. It's the sheriff. He nods at me and tips his hat. Once he's out of the village, he speeds up a bit. I head in the same direction and wonder who he's going to visit.

In the distance, I see Kate's tent. I follow the path full of ruts. To my surprise, I see the sheriff stop at our tent. He dismounts, and I see Kate come out. As quickly as I can, without slipping on the icy snow, I hurry home. Kate sees me coming and points in my direction. My curiosity grows, but so does my unease. Questions swirl in my mind. What's the sheriff doing at our place? Has something terrible happened back home in Vancouver?

Kate and the sheriff wait until I am close enough to hear them. The sheriff greets me again and asks if I am Elsa.

"Yes, that's me," I reply.

"Is it true that you helped a First Nations boy yesterday?" asks the sheriff.

"Yes, that's true," I say, surprised. "He was too sick to walk home alone, so I took him there. Is there a problem with that?"

"No, it's good to help your fellow man," says the sheriff. "But you need to know that the boy ran away from the Port Alberni School. The school has reported him missing, and we've been keeping an eye on the family for a few weeks because we suspected he might return home. Yesterday, we received a tip that the boy had indeed arrived."

My eyes widen. "Who gave you that tip?" I ask, gasping for breath.

"Unfortunately, I can't say, miss."

I look at Kate.

"No," Kate says defensively, "I didn't do it."

"Then who?" I ask more to myself than to the others. "The teacher," I say. "The teacher must have said something."

"I can't say, miss," the sheriff replies again.

Then he gets back on his horse, tips his hat, and says, "Once the boy is better, he must return to school."

An idea suddenly comes to me. "Can I teach the boy until he recovers? I'm a schoolteacher from Vancouver. I'm here for a while to help my sister," I add for clarification.

"Do what you want," says the sheriff, not unfriendly, but firmly adds, "once he's better, he will return to school."

The sheriff then rides back down the road toward the village.

Kate and I go into the tent, and I drop the groceries with a thud. "I'm going to school to ask the teacher why he betrayed the boy," I say resolutely.

"Don't do that now," Kate soothes. "I can't believe he did that."

"Well, I can believe it after he made it clear to me yesterday that he fully supports the government's rules."

Kate shakes her head. "I'm not so sure about that," she says softly.

"Since when are you the teacher's advocate?" I ask angrily. "I'm going to the village."

Immediately, I dash out of the tent and head back to the school.

In the village, I run into Fred.

"So," he says tauntingly, "have you been naughty? Did the sheriff come by because you did something wrong?"

"Man, go away," I snap and continue toward the school.

I peek through the window above the classroom door. The teacher sees me and comes outside. He quietly closes the door behind him. "They're taking a test," he explains. "I can only be away for a short time."

"Did you report the First Nations boy to the sheriff?" I ask bluntly.

The teacher's eyebrows shoot up. "Me?" he asks. "Why would I do such a thing?"

For a moment, I am taken aback.

"Then who did it?" I ask.

"How should I know?" says the teacher, a bit annoyed.

I shrug. I don't know anymore.

Then I dare to ask, "Could I get a few textbooks and bring them to the boy so I can teach him something?"

"Sure," says the teacher. "I'll drop them off this evening."

"Thank you."

The teacher extends his hand. "Are we friends again?"

I place my hand in his and say somewhat reluctantly, "Okay."

In the village street, I see Fred going into the pub. Nasty drunkard, I grumble inwardly. I immediately regret it. Judge not, that ye be not judged, runs through my mind. "Sorry," I say softly.

A woman passing by looks at me in surprise. "It's alright," she says.

Despite everything, I can't help but smile.

In the evening, Mr. Jelle comes by the tent. Kate invites him in and gives him a cup of tea. The teacher asks Daisy how she's feeling. She still looks a bit tired and pale but says she'll be back at school soon.

"We'll see about that," Kate says. "First, she needs to fully recover."

"Thank you," I say to the teacher as he hands me the books for the First Nations boy. "Sorry for the accusation I made."

"It's alright," says the teacher. "At least he's getting some education this way," and he points to the books. "I wonder how long it took him to get from Port Alberni here. It's certainly more than 62 miles. How did he manage to survive with all the snow in the interior? Not to mention the cougars and bears along the way. The boy shouldn't have done that."

I watch the teacher as he ponders the boy's circumstances and how it might have been on his journey here. I feel sympathy for him. "It just shows how badly he wanted to leave that school," I say.

"Still, it's not right that he did that," he says. "The government has the best interests of the Indigenous people at heart."

That hits me in the wrong spot.

"How can," I say with restrained anger, "it be good for a child to be taken away from his parents? How can it be good for a child to be completely alienated from his family? How can it be good to only be allowed to go home once a year? Why is there a difference between the children who go to school here and see their parents every day and the Indigenous children who are forced to give up their name, their identity, their culture?"

Kate interrupts me firmly. "Elsa."

I look up at her. She nods toward the children. "Please, remember what you're saying."

I fall silent to avoid confusing the children.

"Sorry," I say.

"You're right," Rose whispers in my ear.

"Rose," says Kate, "stop that."

That night, I hear the ominous drumming of the First Nations people until after midnight.

Daisy stays home from school for another day.

On my way to the First Nations family, I search for herbs. I've brought the schoolbooks and a basket to collect the herbs. Not much grows this time of year, but you never know what you might find. I discover a few mint plants and some sage and place them on top of the books in the basket. Slowly, I make my way down the road. I stop frequently to let a wagon loaded with ore and wood pass by, heading downhill. The horses pull the wagons and neigh as if to say goodbye. The men on the wagons greet me.

Behind me, another wagon is coming down the mountain. "Hey, hold on," I hear the man on the wagon call out.

I turn around and see that the wagon has stopped right behind me.

Fred and another man are sitting on the wagon. "Good morning," Fred greets me.

I nod politely enough not to irritate him, which is quite easy to do with him.

"What are you doing out here on the road by yourself?" he asks.

"I'm looking for some herbs," I reply.

I clutch the basket tightly against me, my arm flat under the handle, covering the books and herbs. I try to shield the contents from Fred's curious eyes. But he lets the horses slow down just enough so he can peek into my basket from his perch. I take a small step back. The slope is steep here, and I can't move any farther.

"Are there only herbs in your basket? Nothing else?" he asks, his tone suspicious. "Nothing to bring to your Indian friends?"

"What do you mean?" I ask as innocently as possible.

"Aren't you friends with those Indian people down the mountain? Don't you visit them regularly?"

"No," I say, "where did you get that idea?"

"Haha," Fred laughs nastily, "keeping little boys away from school, eh? Bringing extra food to those losers?"

I ignore him and try to move on, but there's hardly any space between the wagon and the slope. The other man on the wagon nudges Fred. "Hey, we need to move. We don't have time to chat here, or the boss will get mad."

Fred cracks the reins, and the wagon starts moving again. I stand there trembling. What a nasty man, flashes through my mind. In the distance, I see the wagon turn a corner and disappear. I hurry down the path. I can still pick herbs when I walk home, I decide. Before Fred and his buddy come back up the mountain for another load, I reach the trail to the First Nations camp. I look around to see if anyone is on the road, then quickly head up the trail to the camp.

Faster than I expected, I arrive at the clearing. To my great surprise, the tents are gone. I walk onto the site but see only the cold ashes of the fire. All the First Nations people's belongings—the tents, the cooking pot, the knitting, and the wooden walking sticks—are gone. There is no laughter or giggling from the children, no clicking of knitting needles, and no crackling of the fire.

With my head full of questions, I walk back up the mountain. I go directly to the teacher to return his schoolbooks.

"Where could they have gone?" I ask him.

"They probably went toward Lake Cowichan. There's less chance that the police will find them there," the teacher answers.

I sigh. "I hope they won't be found by the sheriff."

"They will be alright," says Mr. Jelle. "They know the local woods much better than white people do."

I go home and tell Kate about the disappearance of the First Nations family.

For a long time, questions about where the family could be haunt my mind. Then I let it go. I also conclude that the Indigenous people are much better at handling nature than we are. They will be alright.

✣

"Will you come with me to Duncan?" Paul asks. "I'm going to mail my article. You can call your parents and tell them how things are going here."

I like that, so Paul and I ride down the mountain with the grocer in his wagon, heading toward Duncan. In the village, we use the phone at the post office. Paul drops off the envelope with his article, and I ask the operator to connect me to my parents in Vancouver. I get my father on the line and tell him about our adventures on the mountain. I keep everything positive and don't mention that Fred threatened the girls. Mom is recovering, and they hope to visit us on the mountain soon. Dad will inform the headmaster of the school that I'll be staying here a bit longer.

We return to the store where the grocer is loading his wagon. The horse, with the heavy wagon behind it, moves slowly up the mountain. We reach the snow line and climb higher. Fortunately, the path is kept clear, or it would be impossible for the horse with its slippery hooves. I shudder to think what would happen if the horse were to slip, and we all tumbled into one of the ravines among the moss-covered trees. I glance anxiously beside me. The wagon is riding forty inches from the edge. Even in places where the ravine doesn't seem too steep, it still drops about a hundred feet. It's densely overgrown, but I doubt the bushes could stop a horse, a heavily loaded wagon, and three people. At the very least, we'd get a lot of scratches from the brambles—if we don't break any bones and end up with the wagon on top of our heads.

"What are you thinking about?" Paul asks. "There's such a deep wrinkle above your nose."

"I find it a bit scary to ride so close to the edge."

"I didn't hear you complain about it when we first came up, right after we got off the train," Paul says, pretending to be surprised.

"Yeah, well," I say, "it was dark then; I couldn't see."

"Just because you can't see danger it's suddenly not scary, and when you do see danger, is it actually dangerous?" he asks teasingly.

"There's that saying, 'What you don't know doesn't hurt you,'" I counter.

"So," he continues in a mock-serious tone, "is it advisable to keep everyone in the dark about things that might make them worry?"

"Oh, come on," I say, feigning irritation but inwardly amused. "You can't have a serious conversation with you. And yes, I have to admit, it's probably better for some people not to know."

Then, suddenly, he becomes serious. "Do you know what the Bible says about this?"

"Do tell," I say, curious.

"It says," he replies, "that you can't add an ell to your height, and not a hair from your head will fall without your Heavenly Father's consent."

"That still doesn't mean you should recklessly ride along the edge," I argue.

Then Paul starts laughing. "You call this slow pace reckless? What you just can't let go of is worrying about what could happen."

I slowly shake my head and then admit, "You're probably right," trying to keep the conclusion as neutral as possible.

"I won't hold it against you," he says kindly. "No one is perfect, and God knows that. You just have to admit it."

For the rest of the ride, I focus as much as possible on the horse's steady gait.

When we reach the top of the mountain, we get out in front of the grocer's store. We walk home. As we approach the tent, we see Fred just coming out.

My hair stands on end. "What is that man doing at my sister's tent?" I hiss.

"Hello, Fred," Paul greets him. "What's the reason for your visit, if I may ask?"

"You may not ask," Fred responds arrogantly. "It's none of your business."

"Fine," says Paul, "I'll ask Kate."

"Stay out of it, man," Fred yells, shoving Paul. Paul stumbles and falls against me. Fortunately, this breaks his fall, and he manages to stay on his feet. We stand stunned as we watch Fred stride away, taking long steps toward his own tent. He doesn't look back once. He probably doesn't expect Paul to follow him.

Perplexed and shocked, we enter the tent.

"What's up with Fred?" I ask Kate, who's hanging laundry by the stove.

"He came asking if I had found the ownership documents yet so he could buy the land from me."

"Why," Paul asks thoughtfully, "why does he want to buy this piece of land so badly? Does he know something about it? Maybe he knows something valuable is in it?"

"It could be," Kate says, "that Dylan had a significant debt with him. I asked him how much it was, but he didn't give me a concrete answer. The question irritated him. He was angry that I hadn't found the contract yet."

"We need to find that contract," I say. "And don't sell until he proves how much the debt is."

"And," Paul adds, "we shouldn't just take his word for it. He'll need to bring someone else to verify the amount."

We're still discussing this when the children come home for lunch. Daisy watches us from a distance, her eyes wide. What's going on in that little head of hers?

ৡৣ৶

After school, Daisy and Amber head outside into the twilight. I'm curious about what they're up to. "I'm just going to the outhouse," I say, stepping outside to see where they've gone. At first, I don't spot them, but then I hear quiet talking and some low grumbling. Carefully, I follow the sound. I soon see a hunched figure hard at work—it looks like someone is digging. I move closer and suddenly stumble upon the two girls huddled behind a bush, peeking at the person digging. I kneel beside them. They look up, startled.

In a whisper, Daisy says, "He's digging on our land."

"Who is it?" I whisper back.

"It's Fred," Daisy replies softly.

"Why is he doing that?" I ask.

"We want to know that too," Amber whispers.

"Let's go back before he sees us," I whisper.

We shuffle backward, trying to stay unseen, and make our way back to the tent.

"Fred is digging on our land," Daisy says as we enter.

Paul stands up, angry. "What does that guy think he's doing?" he mutters, but Kate places her hand on his arm and stops him.

"Let it go," she says. "We need to find the contract and see what it's really worth."

"Alright," Paul sighs, "I'll go to the mine office and ask for a price estimate. They should be able to give me a rough idea."

Then, it's time for Amber to return to the hotel.

"Daisy," I ask, "shall we walk your friend back to the hotel?"

A little later, I walk with the girls the few hundred meters back to the village.

"Tomorrow," Amber says, "we're going to dig on the land again after school. We want to see if there's anything to find. Maybe we'll find not just silver but gold too," she says excitedly to Daisy. "Then we'll be rich, and," she adds softly, "Mama won't have to be with all those dirty men in her room anymore."

We all fall silent for a moment until Daisy speaks up. "Yes, that would be nice. Let's start looking tomorrow before the miners come out of the mine."

"Girls," I say, worried, "be careful. Fred is a strange, dangerous fellow. Keep an eye out for him."

"We're allowed to search our own land, aren't we?" Daisy asks.

"Certainly," I say, "but Fred claims your father owed him a debt, and he might try to get your land in exchange for that debt. If he finds valuable stones, he might demand a higher price."

"But he can't just start digging if he hasn't bought it yet, right?"

"You're right, but some people are difficult to convince that they should stay away from other people's property."

"We're definitely going to dig on our land tomorrow," Daisy confirms.

By the time we reach the hotel, we drop Amber off at the back entrance.

"See you tomorrow," the girls say, and Amber slips inside.

With Daisy holding my hand, we walk back to the tent. Occasionally, she skips. Children are so wonderfully carefree, eagerly looking forward to the next day and the projects they can't wait to start—like the treasure-hunting adventure the girls have planned.

"I should visit Olga tomorrow," I suggest to Kate. "I think it's a good idea for her to know what the girls are planning." We all go to bed on time, exhausted from the day's events. I hear Daisy tossing and turning for a bit before falling silent. Bobby has long since crashed, that little rascal. He runs around all day, no wonder he falls asleep like a rock at night.

Now that we've heard Olga's story and know Fred is actively searching Kate's land, I'm even more worried. What is that man up to? What happened at the mine? What does he think he'll find on Kate's land? How large was Dylan's outstanding debt? Where has the contract gone? So many questions swirl in my mind, keeping me awake.

That afternoon, I'm on my own—Kate hasn't returned from her work at the hotel yet, and Daisy and Amber are busy digging with the twins. I turn the whole tent upside down, searching through piles of clothes, behind pots and pans, under Kate's mattress, and in the trunk that serves as a storage box. But I find nothing. I do my best to leave everything exactly as I found it.

When Kate comes home, we have a cup of tea, and then I casually ask if she has any idea where the contract might be. She shakes her head. "I don't know. I need to think carefully about whether there's a place where Dylan could have hidden it."

Later, as we sit around the fire, Kate serves the food on plates. After we've said grace and enjoyed the meal that Rose and Jasmin cooked, I turn to Paul.

"Any news?" I ask, curious.

"As I promised Kate," Paul begins between bites, "I went by the mine office this afternoon before the whistle blew.

'I'd like to speak with the director,' I told Dave.

'Go ahead, knock on the door, and see if he has time for you,' he replied, to my surprise.

I knocked, and when I heard a 'Come in,' I stepped into the small office. The director was still at his desk, papers scattered everywhere, with a map of the mountain on top of the clutter.

'Good afternoon,' I greeted him. 'You seem busy,' I said, gesturing to the overloaded desk.

'Yes, no shortage of paperwork,' the director replied, offering a wry grin.

'Is everything going well? Any news I could pass along to the paper?' I asked, trying to sound casual.

'Not much to report,' he said, glancing at me sidelong. 'Nothing that needs to go outside these walls.'

I nodded, trying to figure out how to ask the next question without raising suspicion.

"So, there have been no discoveries on any of the plots of land?" I asked, then immediately followed up with a laugh, "That's something no one would tell me. The whole world would be on your doorstep. It's already busy enough here with fortune seekers who can't seem to find the luck they came for."

The director looked at me for a moment as if weighing his words.

'Yes,' he said slowly, 'new sources are still being found, but that's not always in my control.'

I pushed a little further, trying to gauge his reaction.

'That would be on land owned by individual miners, then?' He nodded. 'You could say that. Some people are cautious. They don't like to show too much of what they've found. There are some unsavory types around here who wouldn't hesitate to do harm to get richer. Some...' He paused, looking me square in the eye. 'Some even sacrifice good friendships over it. And every now and then, someone goes even further.'

Something in the air shifted. I couldn't tell if the director was hinting at something or just talking generally, but I sensed a warning in his words.

'I've got a lot of work,' he said abruptly. 'I'll see you another time.' The conversation was clearly over.

'Thanks,' I said, heading for the door. But before I left, I asked one last thing, just to be sure. 'Is there any way to find out what someone paid for a piece of land?'

'All plots were sold at the same price,' he replied without looking up.

'Got it. Thanks again,' I said, and as my hand touched the door handle, he added, 'Tell your friends to be careful.'

I turned back to thank him, but he didn't seem to notice, his attention already back on the piles of paperwork. I closed the door softly behind me, the weight of his words lingering. As I walked back to the tent, the mine whistle sounded behind me. I saw the twins and the girls dropping their shovels in the distance, heading toward the tent.

We sit in silence as Paul finishes his story. The tension in the air is palpable. No one has eaten much except for Bobby, who's already finished his plate.

"It's difficult," Paul says, "to know exactly what the director meant, but it does mean that we absolutely mustn't say anything about the stone we found."

He looks at Daisy, who hastily says, "I haven't told anyone anything."

I pull her close and whisper in her ear, "Good job."

"I haven't either," says Bobby.

Jasmin ruffles his hair and says, "You did well, too," which puts a grin on his face.

৩৵৻৶

That evening, I go outside to get some fresh air in the darkening night. Paul also slips out of his tent, and by the small fire burning in front of his tent, we discuss his findings at the mining office.

"They do have a copy of the contract, but they can't show it to me. Kate needs to give permission for that. So, we need to make sure we find the original."

We manage to find it sooner than we expected. I wake up in the middle of the night. I notice Kate quietly slipping out of the tent. She must be heading to the outhouse. A few minutes later, she comes back. I pretend to be asleep, but in the dim light of the fire, I follow her with my eyes through the tent. She goes to the only nice piece of furniture in the tent, the trunk, over which Kate has sole control. She opens the chest, and I see by the faint glow of the candle she has lit to illuminate herself that she is holding a piece of paper. She holds it close to her eyes, but apparently, she can't read it well.

Then, she places the paper back in the chest and closes the lid.

৩৵৻৶

Today, I helped the teacher at school, and the children walk home with me. As soon as the twins and the girls start digging and Bobby leaves to play with a friend, I check the clock. It will be an hour before Kate returns from her work at the hotel.

I open the trunk and move aside the skirts and blouses that are in the chest.

"Look at that," I say to myself in a hushed tone as I push some underwear aside and see a stack of papers. I take them out of the chest and flip through them. I pull one out. This is the deed, I think to myself.

I turn the paper over. Dylan's signature is on it. If Fred wants this piece of land, he sure wants to get rich from it. I need to make sure the paper disappears. I don't want Fred to get rich instead of Kate. Determined, I close the lid of the chest while looking around for a place to hide the deed.

Then I hear someone outside shouting, "Is anyone home?"

As quickly as I can, I stuff the deed under my bedding. I go to the tent flap and open it.

"Hello," the man greets me. It's a neighbour from one of the nearby tents. "I heard that the ladies here are good with alterations. Could you mend these clothes for me?"

"Sure," I say, "give them to me."

With a stack of clothes in my arms, I walk back into the tent. Phew, I thought I was going to be caught. I collapse into the chair with the clothes still in my arms. Once I have calmed my nerves a bit, I start preparing dinner.

Not much later, I hear Kate and Fred arriving. They are engaged in a heated discussion.

"What does that guy want now?" I grumble out loud.

Kate opens the tent door, and both of them step inside. Kate walks directly to the trunk without first removing her hat and coat and opens the lid. My eyes widen. I turn to the pot hanging over the fire and stir the soup.

"I really thought the paper was in this chest. I put it in here last night," I hear Kate mumbling behind me.

Kate rummages through the clothes and other items in the chest.

"I don't see it anywhere," Kate says, distressed.

"What do you mean?" Fred asks. "You've lost the deed again? You can't be serious. I'll have a look."

He steps farther into the tent and stands next to Kate by the chest. He bends over and picks up a stack of clothes.

"Hey," says Kate, "you can't do that, those are my things. I can look for it myself."

She pushes the lid down. Fred quickly pulls his hands back before they get trapped between the lid and the chest.

"I'll let you know if I find the paper," Kate says firmly.

Fred hesitates, clearly reluctant to leave without the deed.

Kate repeats, "I'll let you know if I find it." She walks to the tent door and opens it.

Fred gets the hint and steps back out of the tent. "I'll pick you up at the hotel tomorrow. Make sure you have the paper with you."

Kate nods and closes the tent flap in his face.

"Ugh," I say once he's gone. "What a creep. Why does he need the deed so badly?"

"He wants to give me a good price for the land," Kate replies.

"Oh," I say, "so you want to sell it without first properly finding out what Dylan's debts were and what the actual value of the land is? Why does he want the land so badly? Did he tell you?"

"No," says Kate, "but maybe he's right that it's here no place for women. It might be better to go back to Vancouver and find a job there. It's certainly much more comfortable than here on the mountain with all the dust, mud, and the danger of mine collapses. Don't you think it would be better for the children to grow up in a more civilized environment?"

"It's everywhere something," I sigh. "But it's unreasonable to sell the land without knowing its true value and any outstanding debts."

"I wonder where that paper could be," Kate says nervously. "Without the deed, we can never leave; I won't have the money to start somewhere new." She starts rummaging through the trunk again.

The twins, the girls, and Bobby come in, and Kate stops searching.

"Mom," Daisy asks, "can Amber stay for dinner?"

Kate agrees, and soon, we're all gathered around the fire in the middle of the tent. After dinner, Kate and I clean up.

Paul is playing checkers with Bobby. They're having a great time, laughing loudly and accusing each other of cheating. Rose and Jasmin have picked up their knitting, both working on sweaters and chatting softly with each other.

"Actually," Kate says, placing the washed dishes on the drying rack, "I'd like to know what's on our land. Dylan and Fred were digging there before the mine exploded and collapsed."

"Yes," I reply, "it would be good to know if there's anything valuable on the land before you decide whether to sell it."

The next day, I'm busy in the tent preparing dinner when I hear Kate and Fred arguing outside. I was home late because I helped Teacher Jelle prepare for tomorrow. Rose and the girls were digging when I got home. I wonder where they hid when they saw Fred coming.

"I told you I can't find the deed," I hear Kate snap.

Suddenly, I feel a surge of courage or perhaps recklessness, and I step outside the tent. "Deed?" I ask. "What do you need that for?"

"Mind your own business," Fred warns me, his tone threatening.

I stand my ground, staring at Fred, unsure why I'm so resolute or where I'm getting the nerve from.

Fred, holding a shovel in his hand, sticks it into the ground with a sharp, deliberate motion, the metal sinking into the earth with a thud just in front of his feet. "I made a fair offer to buy this piece of land from Kate," he says.

I remain silent, waiting to see if he has more to say. The silence seems to unnerve him, and he begins rambling about the debt Dylan owed him and how it's about time to repay him. He goes on about how it should be against their consciences to delay it for so long. "And how impossible it is for a woman to live here in a tent in the cold. And how women can't take care of themselves at all because that's just not how they're made. Women are made to be subordinate to men and do what they're told. That's their place, according to God. They must be submissive."

He takes a breath, then continues: "Women with children can't earn enough. It's bad to neglect your children. I know this from my own parents, who made a mess because they were always busy with other things—work, charity— because of that, they forgot their own son."

I stare at him, trying to stay calm as he becomes more worked up. When he pauses to catch his breath, I seize the moment to make a proposal.

"I suggest," I begin, "that you put in writing what you're offering for the land and the specifics of my brother-in-law's debts. That way, Kate can make an informed decision. And about those debts," I add, "you'll, I assume, provide the necessary proof?"

Fortunately, Paul arrives, because my last remark has struck a nerve with Fred. He turns red, lifts his shovel, then lowers it again when he sees Paul approaching.

"Is that agreed then?" I ask.

Without answering, Fred strides off toward his own tent.

"Did you have to say all that?" Kate asks reproachfully.

"Tell me what's going on," Paul says, prompting Kate to recount the conversation with Fred.

"Those questions were reasonable, weren't they?" Paul asks Kate.

"Reasonable? She was provoking him. He might end up doing us harm," Kate replies.

"We're all concerned about that," Paul says, looking from Kate to me and back. "We've seen what the girls have found. There's likely more to extract from your land. With Fred growing more insistent and angrier, we need to take measures to protect ourselves from him."

We head into the tent. Kate sits on the chair, nervously wringing her hands.

"Kate," I begin cautiously, "what will you do if you find the deed? Are you planning to sell the land to Fred, even now that you know it might be worth much more, and you're still unsure about Dylan's debts to him?"

Kate sits up straight and looks at me intently. "You know where the deed is, don't you? Did you take it to prevent me from selling the land? Do you trust me so little that you have to take things from me like you do with a child when you think it'll harm them?"

I see her anger. I stay silent, but not for long. The truth has to come out. "I saw you put a paper in the chest last night. I took it out. I didn't mean to steal it, but someone came to the door, and I hid it."

At that moment, the twins and the girls come in.

"I don't want you to sell the land to Fred without understanding what's really going on. I'd rather see you benefit than let that guy take it from you," I continue.

"Yes, Kate, that's right," Rose says, putting an arm around her sister. "We love you and want what's best for you."

That makes a smile appear on Kate's face, and as we sit around the fire eating, the atmosphere is good again.

"So, young lady," a voice says behind me, "how are you finding the school so far?"

I turn around to see the mine director. A heavy basket of groceries, which I've just bought, hangs from my arm.

"Good," I reply. "A new work environment is always a challenge, but I'm enjoying helping out at school."

The director extends his hand. "Call me James, please," he says.

I place my hand in his. "I'm Elsa," I reply.

"Would you like to have a cup of tea at the Mount Sicker Hotel?" James asks, offering his arm. He smiles amiably, a smile that's friendly but with an undertone of something I can't quite put my finger on.

I hesitate, considering whether I want to be seen with him or if I should go home to help Kate and the twins. Then, a small voice in my head suggests that he might have valuable information about the mine accident and other matters I'm curious about.

I give in. "I'd like that," I say, taking his offered arm.

We walk through the village to the hotel. A few women nod at the mine director, glancing at me with curiosity. I keep my gaze straight ahead as they pass by.

"As the new assistant to the schoolteacher," James says softly, "You might want to greet those ladies next time. You never know if their children will end up in your class and how much trouble they might cause you for walking with me through town."

I look at him in alarm. "Do they dislike you?"

"Not directly," he replies. "But you probably know there are three mining companies on the mountain? They all use the railway owned by my company. You can't please all the people," he adds. "It's a competitive environment. It's not the strongest trait of the mountain residents to work together, especially not those who have invested in the mining companies. That's why we have two hotels, but fortunately only one school, church, and opera house. Keeping everything separate would be quite expensive."

"Sorry, I didn't realize," I say, a light bulb going off in my head. "And because they only have one school, in which they all have a say since they contribute to its funding, I have to take a neutral stance because all three of them could prohibit me from helping at the school?"

"All four of them," James corrects me. "The railway also has a say. The same goes for the church and the music hall. We discuss together who will be invited to perform."

"Good to know all of that," I respond. "My sister recently started working at one of the hotels. Does that make me biased too?"

"Probably. And that you walk the streets with me as well. So yes, you're starting to get quite biased," he laughs.

"I'll do my best to make some neutral friends," I joke.

"Good idea," he says, and we both laugh as we enter the Mount Sicker Hotel.

We take a seat at a table covered with a lace cloth. The director orders tea, which is served personally by the hotel owner.

"This is the new assistant to the schoolteacher," James introduces me to the hotel owner.

The handsome, dark-skinned man extends his hand. "Nice to meet you," he says. "My name is Tony." His black eyes take me in with interest.

"Likewise," I reply politely, introducing myself.

I observe Tony, intrigued by his demeanor. There's something about him I can't quite place.

While I'm still pondering whether he's too handsome or too slick, I hear the director say, "Her sister is the laundress at the Brenton Hotel. Maybe you could use some extra help, and she could work here too?"

I look attentively from one to the other, thinking to myself, But I didn't even ask if Kate could work here too.

But Tony responds enthusiastically, "Yes, I could definitely use some extra help," and then he turns directly to me and asks if I would like to ask Kate to drop by.

"I'll ask her," I say, though I'm unsure if Kate wants extra work. After the mining accident, more people know who Kate is. They probably want to offer sympathy and support her, I tell myself.

"I'll wait to hear from you," Tony says, nodding politely before returning to his tasks.

I take a sip of the hot tea, adding a splash of milk so I can drink it faster. My brain is working at full speed. I'd like to ask the mine director a question so that we can make the right decision about the sale of the land, but I want to do so without raising his suspicion. I give it a try and say, "What factors can cause land values to rise or fall? Is there a specific type of rock that influences the price, and which types of stones are particularly valuable right now?"

"Good question," James responds. "Just discovering a rock doesn't necessarily indicate the presence of more valuable resources. We look for entire veins to ensure that investing in the land is worthwhile. We also operate discreetly because if people see someone from the mining company on a piece of land, it often triggers a rush of offers."

I stir my tea and drink the last bit. Standing up, I say, "I'd better get going. Thank you for the tea."

James stands as well and helps me into my coat.

"I gather from your question," he says, "that you suspect there might be something valuable on your land."

I want to protest and feel I might have been too revealing, but he gestures for me to remain quiet.

"Be cautious of people who suspect something but aren't part of your family," he advises.

"What do you mean?" I ask, both concerned and intrigued.

"Just like I said," he replies, smiling and shrugging his shoulders, leaving nothing more to be said.

I nod. "I'll take my leave then," I say and walk to the door, stepping out into the street.

Outside, I take a deep breath, trying to piece together what was suggested. What does the mine director know, and what does Fred know? We'll need to have a strategy session tonight by the fire and come up with a plan.

"I have a note for Dave from the mine office, with a few days on it when he could come to class to talk about the mines," says Teacher Jelle to Daisy and Amber that Monday afternoon after school. "Would you take it for me before you go home?"

"Yes, sir," they respond cheerfully. "Maybe we can look at the stones in the display case again. We've almost forgotten what they look like."

"I'll join you," I offer. "If it's alright with the ladies, I'd like to see the stones one more time too."

The girls take my hand and together we walk to the mine office.

Daisy hands the teacher's note to Dave and asks, "May we take another look at the stones for a bit?"

"Sure, go ahead," says Dave.

"Thank you," I say, and I walk with the girls to the display case.

Like all the buildings on the mountain, the office is made of wood. Many trees have been cut down to make way for the infrastructure on the mountain, and the wood from the trees has been used to build houses and this office. The walls are thin, and I hear voices in one of the adjacent rooms.

"It's up to you to acquire that piece of land," I hear the voice of the mine director.

I don't know who he's talking to, but then I hear the other person say, "She refuses to sell, and now she's using the excuse that she lost the title deed."

I'm startled. I don't want those two in that room to know that I'm here with the girls.

"Come on, girls," I say urgently, pulling them along. "It's time to go home."

I take the girls' hands and hurry them away. They don't resist. We thank Dave once more and step outside. Not a minute later, Fred storms out. In his rage, he doesn't even see me and the girls.

A few women just coming out of the grocery store look at him indignantly. "That man isn't right in the head," one of them says.

"What's that guy doing at the mine office again?" Amber says with disgust on her face.

I stay quiet and hurry home with the girls. They're digging a bit more in the piece of land behind the tent with Rose. I've impressed upon them to stop immediately if Fred comes nearby. I start preparing dinner with Jasmin, and not long after, Kate comes home.

"It smells delicious in here," Kate says, sniffing the aroma of roasted meat. "And you know what? That nasty Fred didn't even come to pick me up."

"Good for you," I say. "We saw him come out of the mine office like a mad bull when we were there to drop something off for the teacher."

Kate looks at me thoughtfully. "What was he doing there?" she asks.

I gesture toward the girls. "I'll explain later."

Once Paul is home and the children are asleep, I recount what I overheard.

"It's getting dangerous," Paul says. "Perhaps it's time for you to stay at one of the hotels. It's safer there."

"That means," Kate says, "the person helping Fred is the mine director."

"It seems so," Paul replies. "Although he did warn me about people like Fred, so I'm not entirely sure."

"The mine director also warned me about people who aren't part of our family but are interested in our land," I add.

"Have you found the title deed yet?" Kate mocks Fred. "Do you know it's bad for children, especially boys, to grow up without a father? You should think about remarrying," she angrily imitates him. "Does he really think he's a suitable candidate? Never. Fred told me that the girls were wandering around our piece of land and digging there. He thinks it's irresponsible to leave them behind the tent in the twilight. He says it's dangerous with the cougars and bears that roam around here and come out at night. I told him I'd decide that for myself and don't need his opinion. Then that arrogant jerk said women aren't capable of making their own decisions—that men have to do it for them." Kate is getting worked up and is clearly fed up with Fred's unsolicited interference in her life

"What's that guy thinking?" Paul says irritably. "At school, some of the girls were smarter than all the boys. Fred doesn't know what he's talking about," he adds angrily.

"Do you think," Kate says, "it would be wise to sell the land and go back to Vancouver?"

"Girl, no," I interrupt quickly. "You shouldn't do that now. First, you need to find out the true value of the land and the actual debt you owe Fred."

The next day, Paul and I accompany Kate from the Brenton Hotel to the Mount Sicker Hotel to talk to Tony about the work he has for her.

"Could you help with the alterations?" Tony asks as we sit in his little office. "The pile of alterations could be processed a bit faster. I've heard you're very good at it. The girls here will appreciate it. Can you come here for a few hours in the afternoon after you're done at the other hotel?"

Kate agrees. She can use the extra income.

"Great," Tony says. "It's a deal. I'll see you tomorrow afternoon."

From then on, Kate works at the Brenton Hotel in the morning and at the Mount Sicker Hotel in the afternoon. She works until the mine whistle blows and the mines empty. Unfortunately, Fred doesn't give up and waits for her outside the Brenton Hotel every day at noon. He's becoming increasingly pushy.

"Oh, girl," Kate's colleague Jane says when she sees Fred outside the Mount Sicker Hotel at the end of the workday. "That guy really has it bad for you. He's waiting here for you, too."

"No way," Kate mutters, stepping resolutely outside. I'm there to pick her up from work and follow her.

"Hello, Fred," she says. "Is there something?"

"Have you found the title deed yet?" Fred asks.

"Even if I had found it," Kate says, "I won't show it to you until you provide a written statement of the debt Dylan owed you. And don't forget to include the proof, as I've mentioned before."

Fred clenches his fists, grits his teeth, and shakes his head in anger. Restraining himself, he asks how her day has been.

"Good," I hear her reply, and then she turns and walks back into the hotel, leaving him outside. I watch as Fred takes a deep breath, holds it as long as he can, and then storms off toward his tent. I follow him with my eyes and see Paul walking from the tents toward the hotel.

"I'll get you yet," Fred shouts at Paul, raising his fist in the air.

"What was that about?" Paul asks as he approaches the hotel.

"That man is just crazy," I say. "Kate won't give in to him, and he's acting like a spoiled little child."

"It's time we find out what's going on with that piece of land," Paul says resolutely.

ာ‌ာ

Still, Fred doesn't let himself be discouraged. The following day, he waits for Kate again outside the Brenton Hotel, where Olga and Amber live. For Kate's peace of mind, I walk with her on the days I don't help at school. We ignore Fred and head toward Tony's hotel. I stand behind the curtains at the hotel window, observing as Tony and Jane join me.

"He looks really angry again today," Jane says.

"Yep," Tony agrees. "Everyone's always done it—his parents, his bosses, and now Kate, who won't give him attention."

"Do you think that's the issue?" Jane asks.

"Absolutely," Tony confirms. "I've known him since our gold-seeking days in Klondike. I chat with him now and then, mostly to calm him down rather than to be friends."

Tony returns to work, leaving Jane and me at the window. Jane opens the window to shake out a dust cloth one more time.

A little later, Tony re-enters the hall. "Your husband was friends with Fred, wasn't he? They fought together in the Boer War, right?" he asks Kate, who is carrying a load of mending through the hall.

"That's right," Kate responds. "They grew up together and went to the same school."

"I know Fred has quite a temper. If he bothers you too much, let me know. It's hard to see a beautiful woman like you being harassed by a man like Fred." He places a comforting hand on Kate's shoulder. "You've been through enough."

Kate blushes under the scrutiny of his dark eyes. A warm red colours her cheeks.

"Okay, thanks," she says shyly.

Then he lets her go.

"I believe he likes you," Jane nudges her, having also observed the scene.

"Are you crazy? He's just being sympathetic about what I went through recently."

"Girl, didn't you see how he looked at you and how he put his hand on your shoulder? He never does that with me!"

Kate blushes again.

"He's a nice man," Jane continues. "He runs a busy hotel and is on good terms with the mine owners. What more could you want?"

Kate shrugs. "I'm not sure I want to think about a new relationship right now."

"Understandable," Jane says. "But what is a single woman supposed to do on this muddy mountain?"

"I have my children, Elsa, and the twins," Kate says, glancing at me. "We manage just fine."

"I believe that," Jane agrees. "But Elsa will probably get married someday, too, right?" She looks at me and adds with a mischievous grin, "What about Paul, the journalist? He's not blind and seems like a nice guy."

Kate looks at her, somewhat defeated. "You're probably right. I shouldn't just think of myself but also of my children."

"Well, our boss could be a good choice, as long as you don't start bossing me around," Jane jokes.

In the evening, when the children are asleep, Kate tells me that she saw Fred and the mine director visit Tony that afternoon. "I don't know what to make of it. Could Tony be involved in the plot, too?"

214

"Try to find out from Tony what this means," Paul suggests. Kate nods. "I'll keep my eyes and ears open."

At lunchtime, as I'm about to go home from school to eat, Olga is waiting for me at the school gate. Paul is accompanying Kate to the Mount Sicker Hotel today.

"I want to tell you something," she says. "It might be important."

"What is it?" I ask, curious.

"Last night, Fred was in the hotel where I work. He was at the bar with Tony. Tony doesn't often come to us; he's busy enough with his own hotel. I discreetly walked by behind them to hear what they were saying. They were arguing about Kate. I had to laugh secretly and told one of the other girls, 'Why would they be fighting over her?' I asked. 'Quite logical,' she said, 'it's rumored that Kate is a rich woman.' I looked at her in amazement, but before I could ask more, one of the guests pulled her onto his lap, and I haven't seen her this morning to ask more about it," Olga concludes.

"That sounds interesting," I say. "I'm sure Kate doesn't see herself as a rich woman."

We laugh about it.

"I thought you might want to know," Olga says.

I thank her, and we both continue on our way.

Meanwhile, Fred waits for Kate every day at her work at the Brenton Hotel and walks with her to the Mount Sicker Hotel. Also, Paul and I take turns doing this. Usually, I follow as a third wheel behind Fred and Kate. Kate is starting to get scared of Fred and tries in various ways to get rid of him.

215

"You don't need to pick me up," I hear her say as Fred imposes himself upon her again.

"Isn't it much nicer to walk together?" he suggests.

"I'd like to walk with Elsa," Kate insists.

"No," Fred says illogically, "you don't mean that. When women say they don't want to be with a man, it's because they mean the opposite."

"I've asked you several times to leave me alone. I want to walk to the hotel with Elsa."

"Oh, really?" Fred says. "Since when do women know what they want?"

Kate flares up. "Of course they do."

"Maybe they know what they want," Fred says, "but they have poor judgment about what's good for them."

We've reached the Mount Sicker Hotel, and Kate slams the door of the staff entrance in Fred's face for the umpteenth time.

The next day, he walks with her again. When they arrive at the hotel, he suddenly grabs her roughly in his arms. "You know I love you," he says close to her ear.

Disgust is written all over Kate's face. She pulls away with a jerk.

Then suddenly, Paul appears behind us. "What's going on here?" he says angrily, and before anyone can say anything, Kate runs into the hotel.

"What business is it of yours?" Fred asks furiously.

"You need to leave Kate alone," Paul snaps.

Fred lashes out and punches Paul in the eye. Fred walks away, leaving Paul stunned. Paul gingerly touches his bruising eye with his fingers.

Paul and I go into the hotel as well.

When Kate sees how he's been beaten up, she quickly grabs a cloth, soaks it in cold water, and places it on his eye. "Thank you for standing up for me," she says.

"Glad to be of service," Paul replies.

Kate and I have to laugh because of our nerves.

"It's getting dangerous for you here," Paul says. "You can't safely be out and about while that man is roaming around."

"I'm not going to let Fred push me around," she says defiantly.

"It's not about letting yourself be pushed around," Paul says. "You need to get rid of him. He's dangerous."

"It's starting to get out of hand," I agree with him.

Then Kate gives in. "Yes, it's indeed becoming untenable," she admits. She inspects Paul's black eye again and places a new cold cloth on it.

Just as Paul and I are about to head to our tents to help the twins with their chores, the children come running up. They head straight for Paul.

"Did you fight?" Bobby asks excitedly. And immediately after: "Did you lose the battle?"

Paul chuckles. "Unfortunately, I forgot to put on my armor and helmet."

"Ah," Bobby says kindly, "let's just think of it as better luck next time."

Kate and I struggle to keep from bursting into laughter despite the absurdity of the situation.

"Paul is so great with kids, isn't he?" Kate says softly to me. Paul and I walk back to our tents together, and during lunch, we report the events to the twins.

The next day, I walk with Kate to the hotel around noon. From the maids' lunchroom, we can see who is entering the hotel. This way, we can immediately greet guests who arrive around lunchtime, so they don't have to wait unnecessarily. During the week, especially now in winter, not many guests come to the hotel. Weekends are busier, with people passing through who want to visit the mining village. During the weekdays, it's mostly businessmen interested in the mining activities who visit.

Suddenly, I see Fred standing in the hall.

"Hello, Fred," Jane says. "Are you looking for someone?"

"Yes," Fred says, "I want to see Tony, that boss of yours," he adds with a sneer.

"Just a moment," she says, and I see Jane walk toward Tony's office.

I stand up and hide behind the doorpost so Fred doesn't see me.

Jane knocks on Tony's door.

"Come in," is called from inside the office.

Jane opens the door. "Fred is here to see you," she announces.

"Let him in," Tony says.

Jane lets Fred in and closes the door behind him. There are a few guests in the hall who are about to go outside. Kate and I come out of the lunchroom and go to Jane, who is still standing behind the door.

"Shh," she says, holding a finger to her lips.

I hear fragments of the conversation taking place behind the door. Suddenly, the voices grow louder.

"It was *my* idea," I hear Fred shouting.

"I have just as much right as you," Tony shouts back.

"Just so you know, I have the oldest rights," Fred adds, shouting angrily. "I managed to get her husband here. I convinced him to invest Kate's inheritance. If I hadn't done that, then..."

I can't make out the rest of the sentence. Kate and I stand frozen, listening. We hurry back to the lunchroom. Then the door flings open, and Fred storms out of the office and down the exterior stairs of the hotel. We jump behind the coats hanging on the rack. Tony looks briefly into the hall and then slams the door shut. He hasn't noticed us. Kate is shaking with nerves. I take her by the arm and pull her into the kitchen, away from the hall.

Then suddenly, the porter storms into the kitchen. "That guy who always picks you up from work is out in front of the hotel shouting," he says, pointing at Kate.

Kate jumps up and follows the porter swiftly to the front door. I follow right behind her. Kate steps onto the veranda with me in tow. Fred is standing in front of the hotel, holding a gun.

"Fred, what's going on?" Kate calls out.

"It's your fault," he shouts back. "If you had listened to me, none of this would have gone so wrong."

Jane and the porter have also come to stand behind us. Faces of guests and staff appear at the windows.

Kate is trembling. "What have I done wrong?" she asks, shivering, to me and Jane.

Then, there's a deafening bang, and a windowpane shatters next to us. Everyone screams, and those on the veranda stumble inside.

Tony comes running out of his office. "What happened?" he shouts.

"Fred has gone mad and shot out one of the windows," Kate says, trembling.

"I'll handle this," Tony says and walks out onto the veranda.

"Are you sure you should be doing this?" Kate calls after him.

"I'll talk to him," Tony reassures her and confidently walks out into the street.

But Fred aims his gun at him. He fires, and when the gunpowder smoke clears, we see Tony fall to the ground.

Fred apparently realizes what he's done. He turns around and runs off into the woods, away from the hotel. Kate and I race down the stairs and kneel beside Tony. Kate cradles his head in her arms. Tony's face is contorted with pain. He clutches his hands to his stomach. Through his fingers, I see a growing bloodstain darkening his clothes. Panicked, I look around for something to stop the bleeding. People from the hotel have rushed out and are forming a circle around us. Everyone is talking anxiously.

"Oh, Tony," Kate says, panic in her voice. "What is happening with you and Fred?"

Tony looks at her. "Sorry," he says. Then his eyes drift away.

"Sorry for what?" Kate asks, confused, but no answer comes anymore.

Several miners, disturbed from their lunch break by the sound of the shots, run into the woods searching for Fred.

The next morning, at the crack of dawn, Tony is carried down the mountain to be buried in Duncan. Because it is too dangerous for Kate, Paul, the children, the twins, and myself to be outside, we do not attend the funeral. Fred is still somewhere out there with a gun. No one knows where he is. We remain in the hotel, waiting for the sheriff and his men, who arrived from Duncan yesterday and are also staying at the hotel, to resume their search for Fred.

The sun rises above the mountains, and the miners who did not go to the funeral are hard at work. A sad, fearful silence hangs over the hotel. An officer walks back and forth on the veranda with his gun at the ready, scanning the lightening mountain.

I feel a lot of unease in my body and keep walking past the windows to see if anything is happening outside.

Around ten o'clock, Fred suddenly appears in front of the hotel. The officer aims his gun and shouts for Fred to surrender.

"Kate, come," I call, motioning for her to come to the window.

Kate puts a stack of linen on the table in the large room and comes to stand next to me.

"I want to speak with Kate," we hear Fred shout. The thin glass in the windows doesn't block much of the sound.

Fred sees Kate and me standing behind the windows and points at us. The officer turns halfway and tries to keep an eye on both Fred and us. Meanwhile, the officers who had been stationed at the back of the hotel have come to the front. The sheriff has also arrived.

"Kate must decide for herself if she wants to speak with you," the sheriff calls out.

Kate steps away from the window and goes to the front door. She stands on the veranda. I follow close behind Kate to support her in whatever might come.

"I want Kate here with me," Fred loudly repeats his demand. "If not," he screams, "then ..." and he aims his gun at his head.

Kate trembles and starts to cry. "He's putting his life in my hands," she sobs despairingly.

"Mama, don't go," Daisy says, having escaped the twins' grasp and clinging to her mother. Kate pulls her close.

Anxiously, Kate asks the sheriff what she should do. "If I tell him I won't go with him and he kills himself, does that make me a murderer?"

The sheriff looks at her thoughtfully.

"Well," she insists fearfully, "do I have to be the one to decide his fate?"

Paul comes to stand with us and says firmly, "Kate, it's his own responsibility what he does with his life. You don't have to sacrifice your own life for him and mentally destroy yourself by living in misery with him. Think about your children. It will be a miserable future for them. You certainly don't want to do that to them."

"Yes, but," she sobs, "I actually decide his future, right?"

"Absolutely not," Paul and I say in unison. "He's mentally ill; he's not right in his head. No one should live like that, and you shouldn't be afraid that you're the one who will kill him. Besides, he will be hanged for Tony's murder."

"Mama," Daisy pleads, "never go with that creep."

Kate looks through her tears into her daughter's pleading eyes. "You have your father's eyes," Kate says. "It's time he gets what he deserves for the betrayal of someone who called himself his friend but threw him into misfortune."

Then Kate takes a few steps down the stairs. "Fred," she calls, "I don't want you to hurt yourself."

Fred perks up. "Come, come with me," he calls back, "I'll take good care of you!"

"Mama, that's not true," Daisy cries behind her.

Then Kate continues. "I don't want you to kill yourself," she calls. "Just surrender, and there might be a less severe punishment than hanging."

"I don't deserve to be punished!" Fred shouts. "You're the one who refuses to listen to me."

For a moment, Kate is taken aback. "Listen to you?" she cries out in confusion. "Why should I do that?" She looks distraught.

"Because," he yells, "I promised your husband during the mine accident that I would take care of you if he died."

I pull on Kate's arm. "Come on," I say, "there's no reasoning with him."

"I'm not going with you," Kate suddenly declares bravely. "You betrayed my husband, your own friend, and you will surely make my life hell."

I see all of Kate's patience with Fred disappear in an instant. She steps back onto the veranda. It is eerily quiet around the hotel. Behind every window is somebody peeking through. Then Fred slowly raises his gun. I hear the clicks of the officers' guns beside me. Fred places the gun under his chin.

"Oh no," Kate whimpers, trembling with emotion. She covers her face with her hands and peeks through her fingers.

I hold her arm tightly, frozen in place.

"Mama, Mama," Daisy says fearfully, "Mama, he's going to shoot!"

The sheriff bellows, "Put down your weapon, now, in the name of the law!"

Fred has never listened to anyone and doesn't now, either. Slowly, his thumb presses the trigger down, and a deafening shot echoes through the mountains. Splatters fly everywhere. Then his body collapses.

We stare at the scene, the blood draining from our faces. My legs feel like rubber, and I can taste my breakfast rising in my throat.

The police officers run to Fred, but it's too late for help. Paul pulls us inside and leads us to a table. We slump into the chairs, our hands shaking.

"Did you see that?" Amber asks Daisy with wide, terrified eyes.

Daisy stares at her, unable to speak. Her head slowly nods up and down in a silent confirmation.

✥

After the blood-curdling drama with Fred, we have a meeting to decide what to do next. None of us wants to stay on the mountain any longer.

Paul wrote a poignant story for the newspaper this morning. "Are you coming to Duncan with me to call your parents?" he asks. "I want to send my story to the Vancouver Weekly Herald. This is front-page news."

"I can do that, as long as Kate agrees," I reply.

"Rose and I will stay with Kate," says Jasmin.

The ride down is a strange experience. Paul and I don't quite know what to say. We're both absorbed in our own thoughts. The grocer talks even more. I try to shut out the hundred-and-one questions he's firing at us. I only catch half of them since we're in the jolting wagon, and he's on the box. Paul responds politely but minimally.

During the phone call, I briefly tell Dad what happened. I try to avoid vivid descriptions, but Dad figures it out.

"Don't tell Mom the details," he says softly on the phone. "I'll inform Fred's parents. I know they haven't been in touch for years, but they need to be told. It's better that I do it than the police suddenly showing up at their doorstep with the bad news."

"Thank you, Dad. That will certainly be a difficult visit for you."

I also get Mom on the phone. With a trembling voice, she asks if we could please come home.

"We'll come as soon as Kate has sold the property," I assure her.

When we return to the hotel, it seems that no one has really been able to pick up the pieces yet.

James, the mine director, enters the hotel's lunchroom. I look surprised and wonder what he's doing here.

"Good afternoon," he greets us.

We greet back and look at him expectantly.

"Could you all," he says, pointing to us, "come to my office, please?" he asks.

We nod. I'm curious about what he wants to tell us. He immediately turns and disappears as quickly as he arrived.

"What does he want from us?" I say, puzzled. "I don't trust him an inch."

"Do you want me to come with you?" asks Teacher Jelle, who has sent the schoolchildren home after Fred's suicide and has come to the hotel. "Maybe you could use some reinforcement?"

"That's a good idea," says Paul.

We put on our coats and leave the hotel. The twins stay with the children in the hotel. I take Kate's arm, and we walk to the mine office, followed by the two men.

"Welcome," James greets us as we enter the director's office under the curious gazes of Dave, who stands at the counter, and the secretary, who has her desk across from him. He closes the door as we step inside. The office is cramped, with only two chairs in front of the director's desk. Paul and Jelle offer Kate and me the chairs and stand behind us.

"Kate," the director begins, "Fred made you several offers to buy your land. He did this in cooperation with me. Fred owed me a large sum. Your husband owed Fred money. Fred planned to buy your land and then sell it to me for a price that would clear his debt to me. Now that Dylan is no longer here and Fred has committed suicide, I want to make you a direct offer. I want to buy your land." He pauses and looks at Kate intently.

"Why?" Kate asks, trembling. "Are there still debts to settle? Now that Fred is gone, I surely don't owe him anything anymore, right? Or do I now owe you?" she asks, suddenly frightened. "Debt doesn't transfer that way, does it?"

"No," he says, to her relief. "Fred's debt was nullified by his death, and I cannot claim your husband's debt."

The director then names the amount he wants to offer for Kate's land.

Kate stares at him, and I, too, am blown away by the idea of such a huge amount.

"You must see potential in the land if you're offering that much for it," Paul says, who has been silent until now.

"Yes," says the director, "I think it has a lot of potential, although I want to send a land surveyor to check it. When your husband bought the land, he bought two plots at once—the land you live on, and Fred's land. When your husband bought the land, he told me he wanted to invest your inheritance money wisely. He did that, but Fred was jealous and made it very difficult for him. Fred said that Dylan's debt to him was larger than the rent your husband owed. Your husband knew better but couldn't stand up to that roughneck. In the mine, at the time of the explosion, they were arguing about it and thus missed the chance to get away in time."

The conversation with Henry and the boy in the pub suddenly comes back to my mind, clear as day.

"Why did Henry suddenly leave? Do you know anything about that?" Paul asks.

"I think he just had enough of Fred and the whole mining situation. I don't know anything else about him."

"And what was Tony's role, the hotel owner?" asks Teacher Jelle. "I heard he was also involved with Fred and Kate."

"I don't know the precise plan of those two scoundrels, but I have a suspicion," says the director.

"Scoundrels?" Kate asks, her voice laced with disbelief. "What was wrong with Tony? He seemed like a nice man. He was at least kind to me," she adds, her confusion evident.

"Well," the director says hesitantly, choosing his words carefully, "both wanted to buy your land, but for different reasons. You know Fred's reason now. As for Tony... his reason was simple greed. He wasn't as rough around the edges as Fred, but he was no less driven. Tony was more... the calculating type, you could say. If you didn't want to sell, he might have tried to convince you to marry him — then the land would have been his, too."

Kate's face goes pale, her body stiffens as the weight of the words sinks in. The realization of what they were both after, hits her all at once, and it's almost too much to bear.

"I think it's time for us to go," says Teacher Jelle. "I suggest that Kate thinks about the offer and lets you know her decision soon. Don't you think, Kate?" asks the teacher.

Kate looks at him gratefully and nods. Then we leave the office. Outside, we stand in front of the building for a moment.

"Wow," Kate says, her voice filled with disbelief. "I really need to think about this."

Arm in arm, seeking comfort and support from each other, we walk back to the hotel, ignoring the curious stares of those around us.

That evening, we gather in the tent for another "war council" by the fire. Kate has convinced Olga and Amber to join us for dinner, which the twins have prepared. Paul and Teacher Jelle are there too. With ten people, the tent is a bit crowded, but it feels warm and cozy.

"I think," Kate says, taking a deep breath, "that selling the land is the best option. That way, I'll have enough money to return to Vancouver and buy a small house there. Olga, I'd love for you to come with me and find a decent job in Vancouver."

Olga's eyes light up with excitement. Amber grabs her arm. "I've been praying for another job for you, and now you're getting it!" she whispers, though loud enough for everyone to hear. Smiles spread across our faces.

Kate decides to investigate the value of the property thoroughly. Paul is tasked with checking the land for valuable stones, and he gets to work right away. The following evening, at the next meeting, he reports back.

"I have good news," Paul says, his voice upbeat. "I walked around and dug in the land with an inspector from the mining company. While there might not be much, there's enough to make a decent profit."

Paul concludes that the mine director's proposed price aligns with the inspector's findings. The next day, we head to the mine office again with Paul and Teacher Jelle.

After some back-and-forth conversation, the mine director finally signs the papers that finalize the transfer of the land. We all leave the office feeling relieved.

As we walk out, I hear Dave talking to the secretary behind me. "Do you get it?" he says. "They've been through so much lately, but they're still happy. I wonder why."

I smile and glance up, grateful for the moment. A sunbeam breaks through the grey clouds, and I squint my eyes, watching as stars seem to dance across the sky.

"It's time for me to go back to Vancouver," Paul says as we sit down for dinner that evening.

On moving day, we fold up the beds and pack the rest of the household items into Kate's trunk. We leave the tent standing. Teacher Jelle knows of a new mining family who wants to take it over along with the wood left behind on the land. I hope they'll get started faster than Dylan and Fred did.

All of us, except for Teacher Jelle, head back to Vancouver.

"Can you put in a good word for me with the headmaster at your school?" teacher Jelle asks as we stand by the grocer's wagon that will take us to the train in Duncan. "Since I've heard the mine yields are decreasing, I think it's a good idea to look for another job."

"I'll do that," I say, taking the letter for the headmaster from him.

Teacher Jelle shakes Kate's hand. "All the best, and hopefully, we'll see each other again," he says.

I notice him taking Kate's hand in both of his in an intimate gesture. I stare at the scene, slightly surprised. Did I miss something in all the chaos of the past weeks? Before I can dwell on it, my attention shifts to the children, and I let the thought go for the moment.

While waiting for the train at the Duncan station, Paul and I call home to let everyone know we're on our way. Dad promises to inform Paul's grandmother. The journey home is smooth but tiring. Dad picks us up from the ferry, eager to hear about our experiences.

"Just leave that part out when you tell Grandma the story," he says to Bobby as he describes Fred's gruesome death.

When we get home, we're greeted with tea and a delicious piece of apple pie that Sarah baked for the occasion.

Mom is in disbelief at everything that has happened and wipes away many nervous tears.

"I'm going to look for a suitable house for you tomorrow," Dad says to Kate. "A house that's big enough for you and the children but also for Olga and Amber."

"I'm so grateful to you," Olga says, her eyes filling with tears.

Mom hugs Olga and Amber warmly. "Welcome home, my new daughter and granddaughter."

"Cheers," Dad says as he raises his teacup. "To a new beginning!"

We all agree wholeheartedly, clinking our cups together.

༄

As promised, I deliver Teacher Jelle's letter to the headmaster when I return to school.

"I'll keep this in mind," he says after reading the letter.

That afternoon, Paul comes to pick me up from school.

"Have you not seen enough of me these past few weeks?" I tease.

"No," he says thoughtfully. "I think I'd like to see you every day from now on."

A smile spreads across my face. "I'd like that too," I say slowly, my heart warming.

"Well," he says with a grin, "then I'll have to pick you up from school as often as possible and walk you home."

"But…" I say, suddenly serious and a little sad, "what will happen if you're sent off again by the newspaper to some remote Canadian area or a distant foreign land?"

"I've arranged that with my boss. I've got a job here in Vancouver for an indefinite period."

I hold his arm a little tighter, the tension easing from my chest. I would love to skip along like Lili, who is hanging onto my other arm. "Look at how beautifully the sun shines on the first new spring green," I say.

Paul laughs softly, pulling my arm closer through his. "It's a beautiful sight, isn't it?"

"Tada!" Rose calls as she bursts into the living room, waving a letter.

"A letter for Kate. Guess who it's from?"

Everyone stops what they're doing and looks curiously at the fluttering letter.

Kate stands up. "Let me see it," she says.

"First guess," Rose teases playfully.

"Rose," Dad intervenes, "give the letter to Kate, will you?"

Rose pouts but hands the letter over to Kate. She turns it over to see where it's from.

"It was posted in Duncan," she says nervously. "It's from Teacher Jelle."

Rose nudges Jasmin, nearly making her fall off her chair.

"I thought so," Rose whispers in Jasmin's ear. "He likes her."

"What does he write?" Mom asks, and Kate rips open the letter.

Her eyes dart over the lines. "He's gotten a job here at the school. He's moving to Vancouver!"

"What?" I say, surprised. "Why didn't the headmaster tell me? Why is he always so secretive?"

No one listens to me, and everyone starts chattering excitedly.

"He's coming next week," Kate says. "He's asking if we might know of a place for him to live."

"Well, that works out nicely," Dad says. "Next week, you, Olga, and the children will move into your own house. Then he can stay here until he finds something more suitable."

I grumble a bit more about the headmaster.

"Hey, Elsa," Jasmin whispers, "don't get worked up. In a while, when you marry Paul, you'll have to quit your job at school anyway. You can put up with that headmaster for now."

"That's true," I say. "It's better to accept some situations you can't change."

Epilogue

The fire on Mount Sicker has been brought under control by the firefighters, and fortunately, no one was injured. I haven't heard anything about new discoveries of precious metals that might reignite a gold rush.

It's Saturday, and it promises to be a beautiful day. The sun shines in a clear blue sky, and Warmland Valley lives up to its name. The heat from the warmed earth lingers between the mountains for a long time.

On my way back from the supermarket, I spot an elderly First Nations woman sitting on a low garden stool at the corner of Trunk Road. She's carving a piece of wood with a sharp knife. Several small figures are already lying on the ground in front of her. When the traffic light turns green, I make a U-turn and park my car in the lot next to the intersection.

I walk over to the old woman. Around her are wooden figures, knitted hats and socks, a spear for catching salmon, and a metal detector.

"Good morning," I greet her. "What are you making?"

She looks up briefly, picks up a small figure from the ground, and shows it to me. I take it and examine the grinning face of a miniature totem pole. I turn it around; the wood is painted red and black in several spots.

I point to the metal detector next to her stool. "Have you ever found gold?" I ask.

She looks at me silently, her eyes narrowed. She assesses whether she can trust me and then says, "Sometimes." She nods in confirmation.

I don't press her further; I don't expect she will say more.

A First Nations man, around 25 years old, arrives with a small boy.

"Hello, Grandma," the boy says, giving his grandmother a hug.

The young man picks up the metal detector and the spear. "Come on," he says to the boy, "we're going."

"Yes!" the boy cheers. "Grandma, we're going spearfishing, and I get to use the metal detector by the river."

The child coughs and his grandmother says, "When you get home, you should drink some pine needle tea. If you're still coughing like that on Monday, you won't be able to go to school."

She stands up and walks to the tall pine tree behind her. "Here, take this for the tea," she says, pinching a few needles between her thumb and forefinger and pulling them from the tree.

The boy makes a little cup with his hands, and his grandmother places the needles in it.

"Listen to your father, and don't make too much noise. You know, Thumquas doesn't like noise. He sleeps during the day."

The boy nods.

As they walk away, I ask curiously, "Who is Thumquas?"

"Sasquatch," the old woman replies. And when she sees the puzzled look on my face, she adds, "Bigfoot."

"Oh," I say, surprised. "Do you think he really exists?"

"Do I think he really exists?" she responds gruffly. "I know he really exists."

I'm torn about whether to ask more, but then she continues, "I can tell you many stories of people who have seen him, but he doesn't like us to talk about him."

Customers start approaching the old woman, and it's time for me to move on. I buy a beautifully carved wooden hummingbird, the bird that is often seen here. The figure is adorned with green and black patterns. I thank the First Nations woman for the conversation and decide to take a stroll around town.

I stop briefly to read the street name sign for Canada Avenue. This is the road where Kate, Elsa, and the others boarded the train to travel back to Vancouver. Under 'Canada Avenue' is the Hul'q'umi'num name of the street, 'St. s'hwulmuhw Shelh'.

It seems as if, little by little, the First Nations culture is being reclaimed from the Western culture—or should I say, that both cultures have begun to collaborate and come to value each other? I think it's the latter. Duncan's train station is a good example of two cultures living side by side, with First Nations totem poles standing guard beside a historic English locomotive.

I pray for a future where the wounds inflicted by greedy and domineering people in past generations will be healed. Like the First Nations people, I know that to achieve this, we must return to harmony with our Creator and show respect for each other and our beautiful surroundings.

Elsa,

a historical novel

Vancouver Island has a relatively short Western history. A single pioneer arrived on the island around 1850 and lived peacefully alongside the Indigenous peoples who had been there for centuries. The pioneers were busy setting up their farms and caring for their families, leaving them with little time to document their experiences. The same was true for the gold prospectors who flocked to the island in the early 1900s to try their luck.

Nevertheless, some people recorded their stories. These are stories I've been able to find online and read in old library books, such as the diary of a farmer who described the daily struggles in the area around his farm.

One of these true stories is about a gold prospector named Fred. Fred is in love with the widow of his friend, who died in a mining accident. However, the widow has no feelings for Fred and begins courting another man. I've described how this story, set on Mount Sicker, unfolds as faithfully as possible, based on the original account.

I stayed as close to the truth regarding historical events as possible, such as the battle at Majuba Hill in South Africa, the emigration of Black people from the United States to Salt Spring Island, and the establishment of the mining village on Mount Sicker. Through old photographs, I was able to identify the transport and communication methods used, as well as the appearance of the mining village on Mount Sicker.

Anecdotes, such as the one Jasmin shares about the stagecoach driver who was killed when a tree fell across the box during a storm, are true. I found details about how Dominion Day was celebrated in the archives, along with information about buildings like Joe Mannion's Inn and the workings of the school system.

The First Nations people have extensive knowledge of the healing properties of the plants that grow in the Cowichan Valley. I attended a workshop led by one of the elder women, where she taught the participants about these plants.

Even today, Indigenous women continue to knit the famous Cowichan sweaters, hats, and socks, which they create on commission for customers or sell in small stalls scattered throughout the valley. They learned the craft from the nuns who established a mission in the valley in 1864. The Indigenous women have passed this skill down from mother to daughter through generations.

Nettie

www.ingramcontent.com/pod-product-compliance
Lightning Source LLC
Chambersburg PA
CBHW020834260626
47169CB00003B/972